WISH UPON A CHRISTMAS STAR

KAREN MCQUESTION

OTHER TITLES BY KAREN MCQUESTION

FOR ADULTS

A Scattered Life

Easily Amused

The Long Way Home

Hello Love

Half a Heart

Good Man, Dalton

Missing Her More

Dovetail

The Moonlight Child

The Uninvited Guest

FOR YOUNG ADULTS

Favorite

Life on Hold

From a Distant Star

The Edgewood Series

Edgewood (Book One)

Wanderlust (Book Two)

Absolution (Book Three)

Revelation (Book Four)

FOR CHILDREN

Celia and the Fairies

Secrets of the Magic Ring

Grimm House

Prince and Popper

FOR WRITERS

Write That Novel! You Know You Want To . . .

WRITING AS K. J. YOUNG

The Dark Hour

Text copyright © 2021 by Karen McQuestion

NIGHTSKY PRESS

ISBN: 978-1-7367888-5-1

For Grace Greene, who once told me written words are never wasted

Over the course of several weeks, Gwen Hayward had worn herself out. She'd let waves of self-pity wash over her, wandered the house in a daze, and found herself crying at unexpected times. All of this had been done privately, of course. No one had seen her at her worst, at least not until today when the mail lady, Julia was her name, came to the door, her knit hat dusted with snow, face etched with worry. "I noticed your mail had accumulated and wanted to make sure you were okay," she said before handing over the pile of five days' mail.

"I'm fine," Gwen assured her, and then, realizing she didn't look fine at all, added, "Just getting over a cold."

"Oh no!" Julia said. "And right before the holidays too. I hope you're feeling better soon." As she walked back to her truck, she turned for a second to call out, "Merry Christmas!" Her tone was so dear and sweet, so concerned, that Gwen nearly hugged her out of gratitude. It wasn't that long ago that she'd been a strong, competent woman. How had she gotten to be such a mess?

It was Dean's fault, of course. For thirty-two years of marriage, he'd loved her. On their wedding day, before God and a church full of guests, he'd taken a lifetime vow, and then, like flipping a light switch, suddenly he wasn't in love with her anymore. Possibly he'd *never* loved her was what he'd said, breaking the news over the phone. He'd waited until she was out of town visiting her sister to drop the grenade. "I think it's best if we get divorced," he'd said. "We've grown apart and have nothing in common anymore." His voice was the same as always, and yet it was like speaking to a different person. A man without any regard for her feelings. Once he'd been her soul mate, and now, less than a year later, he was in the Virgin Islands with his former office manager, a ditzy woman named Shawna.

Of all the women in the world, it had to be Shawna.

After he'd hired the new office manager, he'd told Gwen countless stories, all of which had put the woman in a bad light. Simple Shawna, he'd called her. According to Dean, Shawna was so uninformed she didn't know that residents of Puerto Rico were US citizens. So dimwitted that basic mathematics went beyond her. So slow that children's jokes went over her head. And if that wasn't enough, parking between the lines was a foreign concept to Shawna and accessing her voice mail was beyond her capabilities. Her husband's anecdotes about Shawna had gone on and on, no end in sight. Dean had related these incidences with such glee that Gwen had said, "You're terrible. I hope you're at least a little bit nice to the poor woman." Dean had just grinned.

Simple Shawna. Not so simple that she couldn't find a way to steal Gwen's husband. *Former* husband now. Shawna had gotten him slightly used, but in perfect condition. Dean had been rough clay when he and Gwen had met, and over the lifetime of their marriage she'd singlehandedly (and lovingly) molded him into the model husband. Only to lose him to a woman Dean had once mocked.

And now the mail lady was worried about her. In a small village like Poplar Creek, Wisconsin, news traveled fast. If she didn't start to circulate among her neighbors, she could potentially become a source of gossip and pity.

How had it all gone wrong? She'd dreamed of moving to this quaint community for years. She and Dean had planned it all—an early retirement in Poplar Creek, a friendly village with charming older homes and an old-fashioned downtown, complete with a village square with a bandstand and a gazebo. She remembered when they'd first vacationed here and both of them had decided that retirement in this quaint village would be ideal. "Like living in a Norman Rockwell painting," Dean had said. They'd gone ahead and bought a house before even selling their old one. They'd been midway through the process when he'd given up on their marriage and on her.

He'd moved out before she'd even returned from her visit to her sister. In the divorce proceedings, he gave the Poplar Creek home to her, mortgage paid outright. He told her she could have all their furniture and everything else too and she could stay in their original house until it sold. "I know it's important to you," he'd said, as if he were doing her a favor, when in fact she knew he'd moved in with Shawna.

She'd dragged her feet on selling their house and had rented from the new owners for a few months more. Finally, she'd moved into the Poplar Creek house at the end of November, following the worst Thanksgiving of her life. Christmas didn't look to be too promising either.

Gwen thought she'd been coping well, but after the move she realized she'd been fooling herself. The new house and all the dreams that came with it emphasized her aloneness. And, too, she'd be spending the upcoming holiday season as a single person for the first time in decades. Such a depressing thought.

Actually, she was thinking of avoiding Christmas as much as possible. Their son, Jared, had promised to come visit, and she was sure they'd exchange gifts and have dinner, but that was as much as she could muster. Maybe next year she'd put up a tree and decorate the house, but not now, when she'd have to do it all alone.

She still sometimes woke during the night and instinctively reached out expecting to touch Dean next to her. After so many years together, his absence left her empty inside.

The only good thing that had come out of this was that Dean and Shawna hadn't chosen to live in the home where she and Dean had raised their son. Instead, they'd bought a pricey downtown apartment, which they'd filled with modern-looking furniture, all chrome and glass, judging by Shawna's Instagram photos. So much for living the Norman Rockwell life.

For so many months, Gwen had hoped he'd come to his senses. She'd pictured him showing up at her door, begging for forgiveness. That pipe dream hadn't happened. The only one who wound up coming to her door was Julia, the mail lady, worried about her health. Poor woman probably imagined Gwen had died.

Gwen thought of all this as she stepped into the shower and then later as she got dressed, put on some makeup, and dried her hair. Looking at herself in the mirror, she felt a little better. Maybe it was a good thing Julia had come to the door. This one kind act had motivated Gwen to stop feeling sorry for herself and get out into the world again. A trip into the village would be just the thing, she decided. She slipped her feet into her wool-lined boots, put on her winter coat, and pulled on a knit beret, then grabbed her keys and purse and headed out the door.

The sunshine was so bright and cheery it was nearly an assault to her eyes, but after she'd adjusted to it, she realized that being immersed in light brightened her gloomy mood. She headed down the sidewalk, her mood lifting with each step. She passed the houses on her block, noting how her neighbors had put up Christmas decorations while she had been busy immersing herself in wine and misery. Her neighbors took pride in their community. Three houses down from Gwen's, an older woman was adjusting a string of Christmas lights that had been hung from the hedge that lined the sidewalk. She had a jacket on, but it was unzipped, and she wasn't wearing gloves. Gwen would have offered to help, but the woman seemed more than capable, whistling as she worked. Gwen smiled as she approached and said, "Good afternoon." To herself she thought, *Well, look at me, acting like everything is fine.*

Let the healing begin.

"Good afternoon," the lady replied, and Gwen thought that would be it, a pleasant exchange with no entanglement, but then she spoke again. "Aren't you the one who bought the old Whitfield place?"

"That's correct," Gwen said, pausing for what seemed like an awkward moment. "The house was so lovely that I knew I wanted to live there as soon as the real estate agent took us through." She gestured to the woman's own home, a brick Tudor. "Your house is beautiful as well. The whole neighborhood is gorgeous." They introduced themselves, and when the woman said her name was Betsy Hibbert, Gwen committed it to memory for future reference. She cleared her throat. "Well, have a nice afternoon."

She was almost out of earshot when the woman called out, "I'm looking forward to meeting your husband too."

The words had no sooner hit Gwen's ears than they twisted in her gut, leaving her speechless. Stopping to tell Betsy that Dean wouldn't be moving in seemed the most sensible course of action, a direct way to put the information out there, but Gwen just couldn't do it. Instead, she turned, mustered a smile, and waved.

She didn't have it in her to discuss her divorce today. And if she was being completely honest, it was doubtful she'd ever be in the right place for that conversation. If only Dean knew the pain he'd inflicted on her.

Gwen left the residential section and headed toward Poplar Creek's charming downtown, so quaint and old-fashioned it reminded her of the setting of a Hallmark movie. She went by the Poplar Creek Café and waved to a little boy kneeling in a windowside booth, his face pressed against the glass. Seeing Village Square Books, she impulsively decided to go inside and look around. She already had bookcases filled with books, some she hadn't read yet but had been meaning to, but she knew from experience that a person couldn't have too many books. Once inside, she browsed quietly, politely waving off the offer of help from a young man stocking the shelves.

Other customers milled around the store, most of them carrying a few books. Chosen for Christmas gifts, presumably.

An hour later, she stood at the bookstore counter, waiting while the same helpful young man, Nelson, rang up her purchase. She declined a bag, tucking the cozy mystery into her purse. Not a gift, just for her. As he handed her the receipt, she glanced out the window behind him at the village square. "You have a good view," she said.

"Yes, ma'am, I do," he said. "You'd think it would get old, but I never get tired of the view. They could film one of those Christmas movies here."

Gwen nodded. "They certainly could." She gestured toward a decorated pine tree situated by the store's front window. It was covered with stars cut from varying shades of colorful construction paper. "Interesting Christmas tree. Most stores hang ornaments for sale."

Nelson grinned. "We have one of those in the back of the store. This one is just for Christmas wishes." Seeing Gwen's look of confusion, he clarified. "For the children? Some families around here are really struggling financially, so the store started a Christmas wishes program a few years ago. Each child puts down the name of a book they'd love to receive. We assign each child a number, which the store keeps track of, and customers get a chance to give a book anonymously. If you're interested, you can take a star, find the book, and bring it up to the counter to purchase it. We'll wrap it and make sure the child gets their gift. The parents tell us that the kids get so excited. It's really fun to know we're doing something as a community to brighten a child's holiday. If you want to take a look, you'll see how it works."

"What a great idea!" Gwen said, stepping aside for the next

customer, a burly man who walked with a cane. She stepped over to the tree and took it all in. The stars were the size of her palm and covered with book titles. Some of them were in a child's handwriting, while others looked as if a parent had written the words. Each star had a book title, author name, and a number listed. She smiled as she read.

Charlotte's Web by E. B. White #47

Hatchet by Gary Paulsen #93

Coraline by Neil Gaiman #2

Harry Potter and the Chamber of Secrets by J. K. Rowling #132

Any of the Magic Tree House books by Mary Pope Osborne #22

She walked around the side of the tree and kept reading, title after title of wonderful books, some of which she herself had read, others that she remembered from her son's childhood. It would be difficult to pick just one.

As the door opened, the paper stars fluttered from the draft. She glanced out the window, aware that she still had a walk home. She'd come back tomorrow and buy some books for the kids when she had time to linger and could make some good choices. She had a surge of joy just thinking about a boy or girl ripping open the wrapping paper and seeing the book they'd coveted. And to think she could make this happen.

After walking out of the store, she stopped on the sidewalk, taking in the view. The village square looked like a scene from another century. The first time she'd seen it she'd fallen in love with Poplar Creek. She'd had a vision of living there, a place where people were friendly but not intrusive. She'd envisioned going to lunch at the local café and volunteering for the historical society. The house, too, had been part of her imaginings. Iced tea on the porch in the summer. A cup of hot tea while sitting in front of the fireplace in winter while she read an engrossing novel. Poplar Creek had seemed magical.

She could use some magic right about now.

And if not magic, she'd settle for something good.

Out of the corner of her eye, she spotted movement in the bookstore, near what she now thought of as the Christmas wish tree. She glanced over and saw a little girl with shoulder-length brown hair, wearing a blue puffy jacket. With her back toward Gwen, she stood up on her tippy-toes and fastened a star to one of the higher branches. When done, she stepped back and, with her head tilted to one side, gave it a long look. A second later, as if hearing her name called, she turned her head, then left her spot and went farther into the store, out of sight.

This little girl's star was different from the others. It was bright yellow, and the points were precise. It also hung from a thin cord rather than a piece of yarn. By the way the girl deliberately went to the back of the tree, Gwen surmised that this particular star had not been sanctioned by the store. Apparently, the child had come up with her own version and snuck it onto the tree.

You had to admire a child who dared to break the rules. Gwen turned to go back into the store. She had to see what was printed on that star.

2

Walking around the tree, Gwen went right to the spot where she'd seen the little girl hang her star. Even though the child had risen up on her toes, Gwen didn't have to reach very high to take the star from the branch. She sidled out from between the tree and the window to take a closer look. The paper ornament in her hand was an origami star. On the back she saw that something had been written in childish printing. The words *wish* and *Christmas* stood out, but the way it was folded made it impossible to see the complete message. She carefully unfolded it.

Inside, it said, *I wish for a washer and dryer for my mom for Christmas so she doesn't have to go to the laundromat.*

This was not what Gwen had anticipated. If the little girl wasn't going to choose a book, she would have guessed she'd wish for something big and expensive. A trip to Disney World, maybe. A new bike (*Do kids even want bikes anymore?*) or an upgraded cell phone—these were the kinds of things she would have expected. From what she remembered from her son Jared's childhood, kids usually wanted whatever their peers had, or what they saw advertised in commercials or online. But a washer and dryer for her mom? That was unexpectedly sweet. It might be that the child just hated having to go to the laundromat with her mother, but there was something about the way it was worded that made her think that wasn't it. The little girl wanted to give this to her mom in order to ease her burden. The idea, so kind and thoughtful from one so young, was so touching that Gwen felt her eyes well up with tears. Well, she hoped that someone would pick this wish and grant the kid's request. That would certainly be a nice thing to do.

For several minutes, Gwen tried to fold the wish back into the star shape, using the folds as a guide, but she couldn't even come close. As she struggled with it, she heard the background noises of the bookstore: Nelson ringing up a purchase and making small talk with an older gentleman, the piped-in strains of "Silent Night." She tried folding it a different way, again with no luck. How was it that a child of seven or eight could fold a piece of paper into a star but she couldn't? Gwen frowned, frustrated, then decided just to fold it up any which way and be done with it. It was sweet that the girl had folded it into a star, but there was no rule that said it had to remain that way.

She was in the process of doing just that when a woman's voice came from behind her. "Fulfilling a wish?" Gwen turned to look and saw that it was Ingrid, the woman who owned the bed-and-breakfast nearby. She wore flowing colorful dresses and large hoop earrings. Dean had said she was an old hippie, but Gwen found it hard to guess Ingrid's age. Although she had white hair and spoke as if she'd witnessed the village grow up around her, her eyes were bright and her skin barely creased with age. Her movements, too, were sprightly. She walked quickly, with determination. She could be anywhere from fifty to seventy. She was one of those people, Gwen decided, who was neither old nor young. She was just herself.

"Excuse me?" Gwen said.

Ingrid pointed to the paper in her hand. "Are you fulfilling a wish?"

Gwen chuckled self-consciously. "Not really. I saw a little girl leave this on the tree and was curious. I'm having some trouble folding it back up the way she had it. It was an origami star. Isn't that delightful?"

Ingrid tilted her head, considering, and then smiled. "A wish upon a star. And the wish is folded inside the star. What a clever girl. Yes, I'd say that's very delightful."

"I don't know if you remember me," Gwen said, extending her hand. "Gwen Hayward. My husband and I stayed at your place a few times. I bought the old Whitfield house, moved in a few weeks ago."

"Of course I remember you." Ingrid smiled and gave her a firm handshake. "How good to see you again."

Gwen held out the paper. "Are you any good with folding, by any chance? I wanted to return it the way it was originally, but I'm having a terrible time of it."

Ingrid's brow furrowed. "Why are you putting it back?"

Gwen felt sheepish. "I didn't really intend to grant the wish. I just felt compelled to see what she had written. You understand, I'm sure. I had already left the bookstore and saw her through the window. She was just a little thing, maybe seven or eight? She had to stand on her tiptoes even to hang it. I noticed her star was different from the others, and I wondered what that was all about."

"I see."

"I couldn't grant her wish if I wanted to." She held out the paper. "There's no name on it."

"Is she still in the store?" Ingrid asked.

"Oh, I don't know."

"Let's look." She nudged Gwen's elbow and then led the way, not even waiting for a response. Silently the two of them circled the store, passing several shoppers, none of them a little girl about seven or eight.

"She must not be here anymore." Gwen glanced toward the door, bewildered. "But I just saw her. Just a few minutes ago."

Ingrid nodded. "Must have left while we were talking."

Well, wasn't that an unfortunate turn of events. If Ingrid hadn't interrupted her, she might have been able to connect the wish with the child. Gwen could have told the little girl, very kindly of course, that the tree was intended for book wishes. On second thought, it might have been better coming from one of the store's employees. Gwen could have explained the situation to Nelson and given him the wish. Then it would be his problem. Gwen held up the wish. "Too bad she didn't put her name on it."

"That's going to make it challenging for you." Ingrid fingered the silver beads of her necklace. "But I'm sure you're up to it."

Gwen felt like they were having two different conversations. "I thought I'd hand it over to Nelson. The guy behind the counter?"

Ingrid wrinkled her nose. "Why would you do that?"

"He has a better chance of meeting up with the little girl than I do. Hopefully, she won't be too disappointed not to get her wish. It's the sweetest thing. She asked for—"

Ingrid held up her hand. "Don't tell me. That's between you and the wish. And now that you've chosen it, it belongs to you. You can't put it back."

Gwen looked for signs that the woman was teasing, but her expression was serious. "What do you mean, I can't put it back?" There were no rules posted about how this worked or she would never have taken one off the tree.

"You said it yourself. You felt compelled to take that particular wish, so now it belongs to you. Kismet. Fate. Your destiny."

Kismet. Fate. Your destiny. Who talked like that? Gwen could almost hear Dean's voice saying, *Old hippie. I bet she burns sage and goes to drum circles.*

As if she'd read her mind, Ingrid said, "Or, more practically speaking, it's now your responsibility."

"My responsibility? As in, I'm *required* to fulfill this wish?"

Ingrid bobbed her head. "Exactly."

Gwen frowned. She was required to fulfill this wish? What had seemed a charming tradition a few minutes ago had turned into a ridiculous obligation. "That can't be right." She looked at the paper in her hand. "The little girl who wrote this didn't sign her name or list her address. How would I even grant a wish like that?" Without more information, even a private investigator couldn't track down this child. If Dean was around, this might be a fun diversion, walking around the village trying to spot a child that age, but by herself it was one more burden. An hour ago, leaving the house had seemed daunting; now, playing fairy godmother to some faceless, nameless child might as well be climbing Mount Everest. Especially with Christmas only a week away. She tried to keep the emotion out of her voice, to sound bright and cheery. "I don't think that's reasonable."

Ingrid gently squeezed her arm. "It's really up to you, but I've found that if you keep a willing heart, you'd be surprised what you can achieve. Just listen to your intuition. It will steer you in the right direction."

"Listen to my intuition," Gwen said.

Ingrid nodded. "You're going to be fine," she said, and before Gwen could ask what she meant, Ingrid spotted someone she knew on the other side of the window, a man in a baseball cap who'd stopped to wave. "If you'll excuse me, I see someone I need to talk to." Ingrid raised her hand to the man in greeting. "Nice chatting with you, Gwen."

After Ingrid headed out the door, Gwen looked down at the wish one more time. At this stage in her life, she was in good financial condition and would easily be able to buy a washer and dryer. That hadn't always been the case. She thought of the early part of her marriage as the ramen years, because they'd literally lived from one paycheck to the next. And then they'd had Jared and all the expenses that came with a child. Since then, though, they'd had two incomes, lived below their means, and invested wisely. Just as planned, they'd reached the point where the harvest had come in. She'd anticipated everything except the divorce. So she had the means to be generous, and she'd gladly fulfill this wish if it was at all possible. But it didn't seem possible.

For a second, she debated putting it back on the tree, or even taking it home and throwing it out. Would it even matter? Deep in thought, she closed her eyes and took a deep breath, thinking it over. When she opened her eyes, the world seemed a brighter place. With a shrug, she placed the wish inside her purse between the pages of her new book. She'd give herself time to think about this. Maybe something would come to her.

When Gwen got home, she checked her email and her phone for voice mail, then set about doing some long-neglected household chores. By the time the evening ended, she'd vacuumed, cleaned the living room and kitchen, and done two loads of wash, all of which made her feel oddly better. Climbing into bed that night, she had the feeling of having turned an emotional corner.

It wasn't until she inexplicably woke up in the middle of the night that she remembered the little girl's wish, still inside her purse, held between the pages of her new book.

I wish for a washer and dryer for my mom for Christmas so she doesn't have to go to the laundromat.

One sentence. What did she know about the person who'd left the wish? She was a child, a little girl less than ten years old, maybe seven or eight. She had a mother whom she wanted to spare from having to tote laundry to the laundromat, which meant they went to the laundromat, an important detail. In theory, if Gwen hung around the laundromat long enough, there was a good chance she'd run into the girl and her mother. Now where was there a laundromat in Poplar Creek? Gwen thought she remembered seeing one a few blocks from the village square.

She could almost picture the building's flat façade with the big windows across the front, but her mind's eye couldn't recall the name of the place, and she certainly couldn't remember the name of the street. Tomorrow, though, she'd search for it online and delve into the matter further. Not that she was going to make this a long-term project. Stopping into the laundromat a few times should more than satisfy the voice of intuition that had woken her up from a sound slumber.

Rolling over, Gwen smiled as she fell back asleep.

3

Marina and her daughter had originally gone to the bookstore to use a gift card, only to discover that they'd forgotten the card at home. Marina sighed when she realized it wasn't in her purse and sighed again when eight-year-old Stella suddenly remembered that it was still on top of her dresser. Lately, Marina had been so scatterbrained. Of course, Stella hadn't remembered to take the card either, but she'd remembered to bring an origami star, which she'd prepared ahead of time.

Walking home from the center of town, Stella had a lightness to her step that Marina hadn't noticed on the way there. She was almost skipping, her brown hair swinging forward as she occasionally cast her eyes downward to make sure not to walk on a crack in order to spare her mother's back. The idea made Marina smile. There were times that Stella seemed so young compared to her peers. When the two of them were home alone, she played with baby dolls, and she also still believed in things like wishes coming true. It was sweet, and Marina wanted to protect her from the harshness of life as long as possible, but sometimes she wondered if she was doing her daughter a disservice by letting her hold on to her innocence for so long. Being a good parent was such a difficult tightrope to walk, especially without the balancing pole of a partner. Ever since Stella's father had died in a car accident, they'd been adrift. Losing Ryan had been devastating, but at least they had each other.

And today, even after Marina had explained that the bookstore's Christmas tree was intended for book wishes, Stella had insisted on putting her own star on the tree. One that had a secret wish inside. A wish that was not a book. Somehow, she would not be deterred. She wouldn't tell her mother the wish that was written inside, and she was insistent on leaving her star there.

Sadly, Marina thought, an unfulfilled wish might be the very thing that shattered Stella's childlike sense of wonder.

"Mama?" Stella piped up as they crossed the street. "How long will it take for my wish to come true?"

Marina took in a deep breath before she answered. "Oh, baby, I don't know. Wishes don't always get answered. It's a nice idea and sometimes it works out, but I wouldn't count on it."

"But some of the wishes get to come true, right?" Stella met her mother's gaze as they walked.

Marina knew that all the book wishes came true. Customers happily fulfilled them, and if there were a few extra that didn't get granted, the bookstore contributed the books. In Poplar Creek, no child who wanted a book for Christmas was disappointed. But Stella's wish, left randomly on a tree intended for book wishes? Unlikely, if not impossible. "Not always," she said gently.

Not hearing the right answer, Stella persisted. "But it happens sometimes, right?"

"Sometimes it does," her mother agreed. "But other times it doesn't. I just don't want you to be disappointed, so don't count on it, okay?"

"I won't be disappointed," Stella said. "Because it's a special wish and I just *know* it will come true."

Marina's heart sank. She looked down at Stella, taking in her daughter's upturned smiling face, the shimmery blue puffy jacket that luckily still fit from last year, and the plastic bead bracelet, a present from her friend Ivy.

Stella had stretched the bracelet to fit over the wrist of her gloves, and she occasionally pushed her jacket sleeve back to look at the words strung on the elastic: FRIENDS4EVER. *Forever.* Stella had no idea how the world worked. Marina just wanted to scoop her up and take her to a safe place where her heart would never be broken. "I hope you know that children don't get new game systems just because they wished for it."

"Who wished for a new game system?" Her little brow furrowed in confusion.

"Wasn't that your wish?"

"No."

"What, then?"

"I can't tell you," Stella said, "or it won't come true."

Clearly, she was confusing Christmas wishes with those made after blowing out birthday cake candles, but Marina didn't press the issue. "Well, I hope it does come true, because that would be wonderful, but even if it doesn't, we still have a lot of fun times ahead of us."

The reference to fun times was a lie, but a necessary one. Why burden Stella with the truth? Especially when the truth was so bleak. Financially, they were at their breaking point. They'd been able to get by just fine until recently. They lived from paycheck to paycheck, but ever since the government had started sending monthly checks, a benefit for Stella due to her father's death, it had given Marina a sense of security. She paid her bills and kept them clothed and fed. Small, unexpected expenses—money needed for a field trip at school, or Stella growing into a new shoe size—could throw a jolt of panic her way, but so far she'd been able to keep up. She still owed money from her husband's stay in the hospital after the car accident, but every month she sent what she could afford. So far, that seemed to suffice. At least they hadn't sent any bill collectors after her.

But all of her financial Jenga was about to come crashing down. Just yesterday, her boss, Mrs. Krueger at Pristine Cleaning Service, had informed her that they were cutting her hours for the next eight weeks. During this time, she'd make two-thirds her usual salary. Mrs. Krueger made it sound like some of the clients had lightened their schedule over the winter months, but Marina knew it was because her boss had hired her niece to work and all the hours were going to her. More hours would only become available when another employee left in two months to go on maternity leave. And that left Marina at a financial shortfall for two months. Unfair, but there was nothing she could do about it.

Since her husband's death, life had thrown challenges her way. First the washer had died, then the dryer, leaving her no other choice but weekly trips to the laundromat. When her car's engine conked out and she couldn't afford the repair, she was left feeling like the world had it out for her. She'd considered selling the house, but only for a moment, then decided to get creative instead.

Cleaning houses had never been her dream job, but it paid more than minimum wage, and often the homeowners tipped her as well. Another bonus? The company picked her up at home in their company van and drove her to and from each job. Getting hired by the cleaning service just as her car had gasped its last breath had been a godsend. Living in Poplar Creek, most everything from the dentist to the grocery store was within walking distance, so going without a vehicle, while not ideal, was doable. She'd hoped to get a car after the medical bills were paid off, but now, with reduced hours, even making the mortgage payment was going to be dicey.

Marina had done the math, and making the numbers work would be a challenge. She would look for a different job or supplemental hours elsewhere, but in the meantime, making much less was her new reality.

She'd buy a lottery ticket if she thought it would help, but that would be money she couldn't spare. Well, she'd just do what she always did—think creatively and try to make what they had stretch. When they turned the corner, she could see their house at the end of the block. *Home.*

"Wait until you see what I wished for," Stella said, taking her hand. "You're going to be so happy, Mama."

"I'm already happy, Stella, because I have you."

"Then you'll be even happier," she promised. "Just wait and see."

The upbeat words of a child who still believed in miracles and wishes. Marina didn't have the heart to contradict her again, so she simply said, "I'm sure it will be wonderful."

✲ 4 ✲

The next day, when Marina's workday was over, she had the transport van let her off at the village square. She waved as the van pulled away, and two of her coworkers saw and raised a hand in return. They were friends by circumstance, all of them trying to make the best of things. Just living one day at a time.

Another day, another dollar.

Usually, they dropped her off at the babysitter's house at the end of her shift. A kind older neighbor named Beatrice watched Stella after school on the days Marina worked. Initially, Marina had paid her, but more recently Beatrice turned down any money, saying that Stella was such a help that she should be paying Marina, not the other way around. If money hadn't been so tight, Marina might have pressed the issue, but instead she'd allowed it. As it turned out, Stella told stories of helping Beatrice fold laundry and shovel the front walk. It did sound as if her daughter was helpful. And, too, Beatrice said she was good company, that living by herself could be lonely at times. "Your daughter is a sparkler, that's for sure," she'd said with a smile. "She brightens my days."

Imagining the two of them together, the older lady who'd previously rattled around in an empty house now keeping company with sweet Stella, kept her from feeling that her life was a total waste. While she was away, she envisioned Beatrice and her daughter making soup or whipping up a batch of brownies, Stella happy and safe. The idea was calming. She could be at her job, scrubbing the tub in someone else's house, and even though this was not the work she wanted to be doing, there was a purpose to it. A little girl named Stella depended on her. And Beatrice was an added blessing who'd come into their life at just the right time. Life could be hard, especially now that her husband was gone, but there were still good people in the world helping to lighten her load.

That afternoon, Marina had given Beatrice a call from the van, saying she had a quick errand to run and asking if it would be okay if she was a little late. "Not a problem," Beatrice had assured her. "Take your time."

This was one errand she couldn't do with Stella around. Marina crossed the road and headed for the bookstore. In the village square behind her, a young couple stood in front of the gazebo, taking selfies and laughing. Tourists, no doubt, staying at the local bed-and-breakfast.

Once inside the store, Marina walked around the tree, looking for Stella's wish. The idea to retrieve the star had come to her just as she was falling asleep the night before. If she knew her daughter's wish, she could put the word out and maybe fulfill it herself. Some of her coworkers had slightly older children and on occasion had passed on clothing and toys. Stella's bike had been acquired in exactly such a way. And if that didn't work out, Marina could ask her parents, who might be willing to give their granddaughter her wish if it wasn't too expensive.

Marina walked around the tree to check the back, the side closest to the window. The previous day, she'd watched Stella's reflection in the glass as she hung the star. It was adorable the way she'd gone on her tippy-toes to hang it on a branch. Marina scanned the wishes attached to the tree, but all of them were the store's standard construction paper cutouts. She reached over and lifted a branch, thinking it might have been obscured by some of the larger pieces of paper, but still didn't see it. She circled the tree again and ran her hand through the branches, to no avail. Stella's origami star was simply gone. Marina's forehead wrinkled as she gave it some thought. Stella had just left it the day before. How could it already be missing?

There were only two possibilities, as far as she could tell. One, the bookstore, seeing that it didn't fit their requirements, had removed it, or two, someone had come along and taken the wish with the intent to grant it. The second possibility was all the more alarming. Would Stella have listed their address or her last name? Marina hadn't necessarily cautioned her against either one, and now she panicked. Kids had no idea how much craziness was out in the world. She probably thought some stranger would leave a pony or an expensive toy on their porch. Stella knew about stranger danger and that there were adults who hurt children, but Marina had not prepared her for this kind of scenario. It would never occur to Stella that something bad could happen in connection with the wish.

Marina's mind was still whirring with these possibilities as she walked over to the checkout counter. "Excuse me," she said to the woman behind the register. "My daughter put up her own star on your tree yesterday." She went on to explain, and when she was finished said, "I came to retrieve it, and it's not there anymore. Did someone from the bookstore take it down, by any chance?"

The woman pressed her lips together. "Not that I know of. If you wait here, I'll check with my coworker, Nelson. He's here most of the time." She left her station and went toward the back of the store. Walking back to the counter, she shook her head. "I'm sorry. Neither of us knows anything about it."

"Thanks for checking," Marina said glumly. Oh, why had she

let Stella leave her wish? When she'd first broached the subject, Marina hadn't seen the harm in doing it. Initially, it had struck her as adorable and sweet, but now she wondered what her daughter had put out into the world.

⚜

THAT NIGHT, AS MARINA WAS TUCKING STELLA INTO BED, SHE broached the subject cautiously. "I've been thinking about your wish, the one you put on the bookstore's Christmas tree," she said, smoothing the covers around Stella's shoulders. "I think telling me might be a good idea. Maybe I can help it along."

Stella shook her head. "I can't say because it's a *surprise*."

"I know, honey, but I'm wondering how the person who finds the wish will know how to find you. Did you put down my phone number or the address of our house?"

"No." Stella yawned.

"So you didn't put down where you live at all?"

"No."

"Not even our street?"

Stella shook her head.

"And no phone number?"

"No, you said not to give people your phone number. That I should tell you if someone wanted it."

"That's exactly right," Marina said with a smile. "Then did you put your name on the wish?"

"No, I didn't."

"Not even your first name? Did you write *Stella* on it? So they'd know it was you?" Marina imagined her daughter signing her name, the intense way she concentrated when writing something important. Recently, Stella had been looping the letters together—her own version of cursive.

Stella shook her head, her eyes wide. "I just wrote the wish.

That's all." Obviously sensing her mother's pensive mood, she asked, "Am I in trouble, Mama?"

"No, sweetie, you're not in trouble, not at all. I just wondered how you thought the person who found the wish could grant it if they don't know who you are or where you live. Don't you think that will make it hard for them?"

Stella giggled. "Christmas magic, Mama. That's how it works. The wishes are magic."

"You really think so?" Marina asked.

"Ivy told me that. Her sister says it too."

Ivy of the friendship bracelet had told Stella that. How could Marina compete with that kind of authority? She didn't think she could. "Well, I hope Ivy is right," Marina said, straightening up. "But if she's wrong and if it doesn't work out, you can always put it on your Christmas list."

Stella turned onto her side. "Ivy is right," she said, her voice tinged with sleep. "I'll get my wish. You'll see."

Fortunately for Gwen, there was only one laundromat in Poplar Creek. According to the website, Lucky's Laundromat had been serving area families since 1989. Gwen sipped her morning coffee and sat at her kitchen table, reading the information on her tablet. They had different size machines, including some large enough to do bedspreads. The cost to do a standard load of wash was three dollars. The larger washing machines were double the amount of money.

To use their dryers, the charge was twenty-five cents for six minutes. What could be dried in six minutes? Almost nothing. She imagined having to pump quarters into the machine continuously until the load was finally dry.

Gwen hadn't been to a laundromat since she was in her early twenties, and the cost sounded astronomical to her, but of course, this was how it worked when you got older. She clearly remembered a favorite uncle telling her that when he was a kid candy bars were a dime. A dime! And the candy bars were bigger back then. But wasn't that the way of life? Nothing stayed the same.

When Gwen was done checking out the laundromat online, she went against her better judgment and clicked on Shawna's

Instagram account. Shawna posted on Instagram several times a day, always with a dozen or so hashtags. The pictures with Dean in them were usually accompanied with #loveofmylife and #luckywoman and #lovelife. This last one Gwen found confusing. Was she talking about her love life or her love of life? Either way, it rankled.

She often dreamt up ways the universe could pay Dean and Shawna back for the pain they'd caused her. If only she were in charge of the world, things would be more equitable.

Shawna's followers left encouraging comments, things like, "You two are the cutest!" and "#Couplegoals."

Looking at Shawna's account made her blood boil. Gwen wanted to leave her own comment, reminding Shawna that Dean had been married when the two of them met, and just as bad, he'd been her boss. Doing so would expose Shawna as a husband stealer, and it wouldn't reflect well on Dean either. But it would also make Gwen look petty. Sometimes being the better person was the right thing to do, but wow, was it exhausting. It would be so much easier to lower herself to their level. But what would it accomplish? Ultimately, nothing.

She could only hope that karma would even things out.

Between the last time she'd looked at Shawna's Instagram and today, the pair of them had traveled to Clearwater, Florida. There were photos of them hand in hand on the beach at sunset, a close-up of them kissing, and pictures of tropical drinks with skewered fruit and umbrellas. Who did she get to take the beach pictures? They weren't selfies, and they looked staged. How self-involved would you have to be to stop strangers and ask them to take romantic-looking pictures? Or maybe they were taken by hotel staff, indulging the couple's requests with the hope of a generous tip to follow. Gwen thought that this public showing had to be Shawna's idea. It certainly wasn't anything Dean would normally do.

In one of them, Dean smiled down at Shawna, who had her

head tilted back in a joyous but decidedly fake laugh. Between the beach and Dean's close-cropped silver hair, they looked like a couple in a drug commercial for erectile dysfunction.

Anyone else seeing these photos would think this was a couple in love, who'd been together for years. It killed Gwen that Shawna had not only stolen her husband but also felt no compunction in putting it out for the world to see. Gwen said aloud, "He would never go on a beach vacation with me." None of it was fair.

Over the years, she'd suggested jetting away to different tropical locations, but Dean had always put the kibosh on her plans. "And do what? Sit around and get sunburned?" he'd responded. "If you want to do nothing, we can do that at home."

"No, this would be different. We could really get away and enjoy the fresh air and sunshine," she'd said. "It would be so relaxing to be on the water."

"Forget about it. I'd rather go on a trip where I can experience things."

She hadn't pressed the matter. Whatever he wanted was fine with her, and if he enjoyed vacations involving state parks, monuments, and museums, then she could too. The trips were fun, just different than what she'd envisioned. And now Shawna, this interloper, had gotten Dean to go on the very type of trip Gwen would have loved. Well, she hoped he did get sunburned. And Shawna too.

Fresh tears sprang to her eyes, and she dabbed at them with a paper napkin. She really needed to stop looking at Shawna's social media. Seeing how much Dean was enjoying himself in his new life was dragging her down, making the pain even more raw. She turned off the power to her tablet and carried it to the counter to plug it into the charger. Enough of sitting around feeling sorry for herself. Keeping busy was the antidote. She'd go on another walk and check out the laundromat.

After she was dressed and ready for the day, she put on her jacket and gloves, grabbed her house keys and phone, tucked them into her pocket, and headed out the door. Her phone case had a flip back with pockets for cards and her driver's license. The case had been a gift from her son. When he'd presented it to her, she'd doubted she'd ever use it, but now she could see the advantages. *Look at me,* she thought, *leaving the house without a purse. I'm like a millennial!* Jared would laugh at that and point out she was nothing like a millennial, which she couldn't deny. It was fine, though. She didn't really want to be younger. Each generation had their strong points and shortcomings, and she was fine with her own.

The temperature was in the thirties today, with a slight breeze that swirled powdery snow around her ankles as she walked. Even though it was a weekday, people were out and about, taking dogs for walks and driving leisurely down the street. She'd moved to a place that would make the Gilmore Girls feel right at home.

When she approached the brick Tudor down the block, the same elderly woman, Betsy was outside again. This time, instead of stringing Christmas lights, she was sprinkling salt on her walkway. If Gwen thought she could get by with just a wave of her hand as she walked past, she was mistaken.

"Well, hello there!" Betsy called out, raising a hand in recognition. "Gwen, right?"

"Right!" Despite herself, Gwen smiled. After such a long stretch of time spent home alone feeling sorry for herself, it was nice to have another human being reach out to her. "And you're Betsy? Betsy Hibbert?"

Betsy nodded. "The one and only. Do you have a minute to come inside and visit?" She pointed toward her house. "It would be nice to have company."

And Gwen, who normally would make polite excuses, decided, *Why not?* "I'd love a visit," she said. She came up the walk and followed the older woman into the house. When they were both inside, she got a closer view of Betsy, who she now realized wasn't that much older than she was herself. Funny how everyone in the world gets older, she thought, while her image of herself stayed the same. In her head, she was eternally thirty-five. When looking in the mirror, she mentally edited out the slight double chin, the gained weight, and the wrinkles. Coloring her hair made the self-deception even easier. Maybe that was how human beings coped with aging.

Betsy offered her a cup of coffee. "Or maybe hot chocolate? I have marshmallows and whipped cream."

"That would be lovely," Gwen said. Again, this was not something she would usually do. Normally, she'd be walking with Dean, and so the offer probably wouldn't have been forthcoming, or if it was, they'd have a ready excuse. Off to a restaurant for lunch or running important errands. The world was made for couples, it seemed.

Now that she was alone, time went at a different pace, and stopping to talk to a neighbor had more appeal.

Betsy left to go into the kitchen, leaving Gwen sitting on a chair in the sunny front room. Once she was alone, Gwen had time to admire the tall ceilings, polished woodwork, and built-in bookshelves, all of it a perfect counterpart to the cream-colored brick fireplace and Christmas decorations, of which there were many. Christmas stockings hung on the mantel, and a large fir tree in one corner was crammed full of ornaments and had a bright star on top. A nativity scene had taken up residence on a side table, and various nutcrackers stood guard on the bookshelves. By the time Betsy returned with a tray of drinks, Gwen's mood had been buoyed. She hadn't planned on decorating for Christmas herself but was starting to reconsider the idea.

As Betsy set the mug on the table next to her, Gwen said, "I love all your decorations. Very festive."

"Christmas is my favorite time of year," Betsy said, looking around the room. "I love everything about it. Buying gifts for other people, decorating, Christmas music, the movies, carols. It lifts my soul."

Gwen nodded. "I can understand that."

"I host a huge Christmas party on Christmas Eve, an open house. Nothing formal—just neighbors stopping by throughout the evening. People bring food, and I serve punch and coffee. We sing carols, and Santa comes and gives a stocking filled with candy and little surprises for the kids. It's so much fun. I hope you'll join us this year." Betsy clasped her hands together.

"It does sound like fun."

Gwen's answer was noncommittal, but Betsy, so busy talking, didn't seem to notice. She was, Gwen decided, a bit of a chatterbox. Within a few minutes, Betsy had told her all about her life. She was a widow whose beloved husband, Larry, had died four years earlier. Together they had three adult children and five grandchildren. Two of the families lived in the area and visited often. "The kids keep bringing up the idea of me moving to a smaller place," she said, taking a sip. "I agree that this is a lot of house for one person, but I'm just not there yet." She kept talking, telling Gwen about her autoimmune disease, the one that made her always feel cold. "That's why I keep the house so warm," she said, pulling her sweater closer around her. When she was done with that topic, she gave Gwen a summary of each neighbor up and down the street.

Gwen nodded politely and kept sipping her hot chocolate. There was something nice about Betsy's view of the world. Her voice, too, had a certain lulling effect, the way she talked endlessly not requiring much in response. Gwen was so much in her own head that when Betsy asked her a question it took a few seconds to register. So long that Betsy asked again, "And how about you?"

"Me?"

"Yes. I'm so sorry. I seem to have taken over the conversation. I'd love to hear about you and your life."

"There's not much to tell." Gwen took in a deep breath and sighed. "I'm fifty-nine. I have one son, Jared. He's not married, and I don't have any grandchildren. And I'm divorced. This happened recently and came as a complete surprise to me."

Betsy looked stricken. "Oh, I'm so sorry."

Saying the words was such a relief that Gwen continued on, telling Betsy the whole sordid story, how Dean had blindsided her by telling her he no longer loved her, then took up with a woman named Shawna. She ended by saying, "I never saw it coming." She took one last sip of her drink. "I thought we were happy. We never argued. We had the same goals for retirement. We were always in sync. We finished each other's sentences. I still can't believe it sometimes."

Betsy nodded thoughtfully. "Sometimes life pulls the rug out from under you. I'm sorry. It had to be awful."

"It was awful." Gwen took comfort in Betsy's sympathy. Even though Betsy herself had lost her husband to a heart attack, she was still compassionate to what Gwen was going through. Why had she been so reluctant to let people know what was going on in her life? Dean's decision wasn't her shame. "Thank you for letting me talk. It's made me feel better."

"Anytime. I know I have a tendency to yammer on," Betsy said, "but I'm also a pretty good listener, so keep that in mind if you ever want to unload."

"I will," Gwen said. "I was actually heading out to the laundromat this morning. Have you been there? I believe it's not too far from here."

"Lucky's? Of course. I've been meaning to take my comforters in, but I keep putting it off." In short order, she gave directions, and even though Gwen already knew where it was, she nodded politely. "Today it should be a pleasant walk from here, especially since you're not carrying any laundry."

"I'm not doing laundry today. Just checking it out," Gwen explained. "I took a wish off the tree in the bookstore, but instead of requesting a book a little girl wished for a washer and dryer so her mom wouldn't have to go to the laundromat."

"Well, isn't that sweet!"

"Yes, it is, and I'd love to do something to grant her wish, but unfortunately she didn't leave her name or any identifying information. My only thought is that I might be able to spot them at the laundromat."

Betsy's face scrunched up in confusion. "If she didn't leave any identifying information, how do you know it was a girl? From the writing?"

"I saw her from a distance. She looked to be about seven or eight, dark brown shoulder-length hair, wearing a blue puffy jacket. Do you have an idea who that could be?"

Betsy shook her head. "Not offhand. That's a pretty general description. You don't have any other clues?"

"The wish was written on yellow paper and folded into an origami star, so either the child or someone in her family knows origami."

"Origami. I see." Betsy nodded. "That's not a lot to go on, but I'll ask around."

Gwen stood up. "I'd appreciate it. Thanks for the hot chocolate. It was a treat, and I enjoyed our visit."

"Anytime," Betsy said, following her to the front hall, where Gwen retrieved her outerwear. When Gwen went outside, Betsy kept the door open and called out, "Have fun with your detective work. I'll say a prayer that you find the little girl."

❧ 6 ❧

Lucky's Laundromat was nothing like Gwen expected. The laundromats she'd been to in her twenties were grim, cramped places, accented with cracked linoleum and ancient-looking machines. In her memory, laundromats were mostly used by college students and struggling young families, and sometimes frequented by homeless people looking for a place to pass the time. The one in Poplar Creek was a stark contrast, spacious and sparkling clean. The tile floor looked new, as did all of the machines. On one side, a wall was devoted to machines that dispensed detergent and softener. Next to that was a money changer for those who had paper money but needed quarters.

A woman in her forties with multicolored hair and large hoop earrings was in the process of transferring a load of towels from a washer to a dryer. At the counter, an elderly gray-haired couple worked together to pair up socks and fold underwear, their movements in perfect synchronization. They talked and laughed as they worked, reminding Gwen of the times she and Dean had done tasks together.

A TV hanging in the corner showed the aftermath of a home makeover on HGTV. From the homeowners' expressions, they were in awe of all the changes that had been made. The camera zoomed in on the wife's face. She had tears in her eyes as she hugged one of the designers for changing their lives. "I can't believe I get to live here!" she said. No one in the laundromat paid any attention to this touching scene.

In the back were café tables with food and beverage vending machines lining the walls, and next to that was a children's play area, delineated by a racetrack-imprinted carpet and edged with containers full of blocks, toys, coloring sheets, crayons, and books. The chairs were all molded plastic, so no one could get too comfortable, but it was still pleasant enough. The place smelled faintly of bleach, detergent, and dryer sheets, which wasn't bad at all, and after walking outside in the cold, Gwen found the warm interior a nice change.

A young woman sat at one of the café tables, her gaze locked on an iPad, a curtain of dark hair obscuring her face. Her right arm was a garden of tattoos, a sleeve of flowers as beautifully rendered as any painting Gwen had ever seen. Nearby on the floor, a little boy about two ran a plastic car around the carpet track. His face was serious as he made the car noises Gwen remembered from her own son's childhood. Did kids instinctively know how to make that engine sound, or did adults model it for them first? She didn't honestly know.

Sidling up to the young woman, Gwen said, "Excuse me?" When the woman looked up from her iPad, Gwen froze, trying to think of how to formulate the question.

"Yes?" The woman shot a look at the little boy, checking on him before she met Gwen's eyes.

Gwen decided to wing it. "I was downtown recently, and a child dropped something. I wasn't able to catch up with her, but I'd like to return it. Do you know of a little girl with dark brown hair about shoulder length, maybe seven or eight?"

The woman frowned. "Maybe. You don't know her name?"

"No, and I didn't see her except from the back, so I can't really describe her."

"Hmm. That's a tough one." She turned her head and addressed the little boy, who was now dumping out the contents of one of the containers onto the rug. Colorful plastic blocks spilled forth. "Dawson! Don't make a mess. You know the rules at Lucky's. We'll have to pick up all the toys before we go." She returned her attention to Gwen. "What did she drop?"

"It was an origami star, made with yellow paper. Do you know anyone who does origami?"

"Nope." She shook her head vigorously. "You might want to ask Lucky, though. He knows everyone around here."

There was an actual guy named Lucky? "If you could point him out to me, I will."

"I don't think he's here today. The place is self-serve, so he kind of comes and goes. You'll know him when you see him, though, because he always wears a baseball cap with the Lucky's logo on it. You might also want to ask Ingrid—she owns the bed-and-breakfast. It's scary how much she knows about the people around here."

Practically worthless advice considering Lucky wasn't there and she'd already talked to Ingrid, but the woman meant well, so Gwen said, "Thank you. I appreciate it."

As Gwen made her way out of the laundromat, she stopped to talk to the other customers, giving them the same story. None of the three knew anyone who did origami. The older couple wished her luck, though, and the lady with the crazy hair said, "You might want to ask Lucky. That guy doesn't miss a thing."

"I'll do that," Gwen said. "Thanks."

A few days earlier, even stepping foot outside her house to get the mail had seemed a daunting task, but now that she was out and about, Gwen found herself not quite ready to go home. An expression came to mind: *A body in motion tends to stay in motion.* Staying indoors in her bathrobe had led to inertia. Walking around in the brisk winter air and talking to others gave her a boost of energy. From now on she would force herself to get out every single day, even if she didn't feel like it. Especially if she didn't feel like it.

She made a point to walk around the village square, greeting people as she went. With each friendly exchange, she felt her spirits lift. Despite herself, she began to smile. And just like that, her mood was elevated and she was able to change her mindset. Instead of feeling discarded by her husband, an almost unbearable thought, she decided to frame it differently. Dean clearly had lost his mind and made a bad decision. As a result, he was now missing out on what could be an excellent retirement with a loyal and loving wife. Whether or not he saw it that way, or ever came to regret his actions, was beside the point. She could control the narrative of her own life, and from now on, she would.

Dean was an idiot.

When she got to the Poplar Creek Café, she opened the door and went inside, almost on a whim. It was lunchtime, and she was hungry. She had food at home, but nothing too tempting. As the door closed behind her, she took in the crowded restaurant, every table filled. She was about to turn to leave when one of the waitresses greeted her with a big smile.

"Hello," she said. "For one today? Or will someone be joining you?" Her nametag identified her as Nicole.

"Just me," Gwen said, an apology in her voice.

"Perfect!" Nicole said, her voice spritely. "Follow me."

As Gwen fell in step behind her, Nicole scooped up two menus off the edge of a table, telling the customers, "I'll be right back to take your order."

Midway through the restaurant, when Nicole paused in front of a table and pulled a chair out, Gwen was horrified to see that the table was currently occupied by a single man reading a book. Nicole asked, "Do you mind sharing your table with this lovely lady?"

"Oh, no," Gwen said hurriedly. "I don't want to inconvenience anyone. I can wait for a table to open up."

"It's fine," the man said, setting down his book. "You're more than welcome." He smiled and gestured to the chair. "I don't bite. Honest."

Gwen hesitated. If she walked away now, it would look rude. Maybe if he just kept reading it wouldn't be that awkward. "That's very nice of you. Thank you." Gwen settled into the chair and accepted the menu from Nicole. Around her she was aware of the gentle clink of silverware against plates and the sound of friendly conversations. Large windows off to one side let in sunshine. She read the menu in a leisurely fashion and finally settled on a salad that looked appealing. As she set down her menu, Nicole came back with a glass of water, ready to take her order. Handing over the menu, Gwen said, "I'll have the grilled chicken cashew salad and an iced tea please."

After Nicole walked away, Gwen found herself face-to-face with the gentleman across the table. His book was facedown next to a baseball cap embossed with the logo for Lucky's Laundromat on the front. Gwen gestured to the cap. "You aren't the famous Lucky of Lucky's Laundromat, by any chance?"

"One and the same," he said with a grin. "How is it that you know me and we've never met?"

"I'm Gwen Hayward. New to Poplar Creek. I was just at the laundromat, and someone mentioned I'd know you by your baseball cap."

He put out his hand and said, "Ben Gallagher, but most everyone calls me Lucky. Not new to Poplar Creek. In fact, I've lived here forever."

They shook, and she took the moment to size him up. He was about her age or maybe a few years younger. His full head of brown hair was streaked with gray and stuck out in classic hat-hair style. His face was tanned and weather-beaten, his expression friendly. He wore a wrinkled button-down shirt. Flannel plaid.

Lucky looked like the kind of man who was easy to talk to. She said, "I was hoping to meet you because I was told you know everyone and you don't miss a thing?"

"Oh?" He raised one eyebrow in such a comical way she almost laughed.

"Yes, I was at the laundromat on a secret mission of sorts." She leaned in to tell him the story of the little girl and the wishing star, her conversation with Ingrid, and her own attempts to work out the child's identity.

Nicole came and presented Lucky with a cheeseburger and fries. "Can I get you anything else, Lucky?" When he shook his head no, she said, "All right, then. Enjoy!" And off she went.

"Do you want some fries?" Lucky asked, pushing the plate in her direction.

She shook her head. "No, thanks." While he ate, she continued the conversation. "Ingrid was pretty adamant that the wish is my responsibility now. And of course, I'd love to fulfill the wish, especially one so selfless. It's heartwarming that she wants to do something to help her mother. I mean, most kids would want something for themselves, but this little girl is asking for a washer and dryer so her mom doesn't have to go to the laundromat."

"My laundromat is not that horrible a place." He grinned.

"I know," she said hurriedly. "I thought it was exceptionally nice. But it's much more convenient to do the wash at home."

"Can't argue with that." Lucky dipped a fry into some ketchup and took a bite.

"Anyway," she continued, "I thought you might know who she is, since they obviously use your laundromat."

Lucky shook his head. "I wish I could give you a definitive answer, but the truth is that I get a lot of families in my business. Sometimes the parents come when school's in session or the little kids stay at home with older siblings while their mom or dad is doing their wash. Sometimes people come in on a regular basis for months and then I don't see them anymore. They either move or get their own machines. I have no way of knowing, really. Off the top of my head, I can think of a half dozen women who come in with daughters about that age. Most of them I know by sight, but I don't necessarily know their names, and I have no idea where they live. I couldn't tell you if the girls or their moms do origami or not. I wish I could be more help." He held out empty hands and smiled ruefully.

"Thanks anyway." Gwen took a sip of her water. "Well, I gave it my best. At least I know in my heart that I tried everything I could think of to track her down."

"I wouldn't give up that easily," Lucky said, salting his fries. "Ingrid is a big advocate of listening to your intuition and following your instincts."

"She told me as much," Gwen said glumly. "I have to say, I'm not entirely convinced."

"And yet, you've started to think this through and even visited my laundromat," he said cheerfully. "I know it seems like a long shot, but I've heard some pretty miraculous stories in my lifetime. People who think all is lost and then something really wonderful happens. I knew a family whose little boy had this aggressive cancer. It looked pretty dire, but then he qualified for a clinical trial for a new drug and it totally turned things around. I knew a woman who met her birth mother using a DNA test and it turned out they lived just ten miles away from each other the whole time. And once I met a guy who was down on his luck and the very next week he won the lottery. Crazy stuff happens all the time. Finding one little girl is a small task by comparison. Why don't you try sleeping on it? Maybe tomorrow something will come to you."

"Sure, I'll do that," she said, but in her heart she knew this was pretty much the end of the line for her. Sometime in the next day or two she would defy Ingrid and put the wish back on the tree. Let someone else figure it out.

7

I t would be nice, Marina thought, to occasionally have a day off that was actually a day off. A free day to do whatever she wanted to do. Twenty-four hours for fun and relaxation without some looming chore nagging at her. She sighed, knowing that compared to some people she was privileged. She had good health, a beautiful daughter, and a roof over her head. It was pointless and ungrateful to wish for more. And yet, she did wish for more. A car would be nice, as would a full bank account to provide a financial cushion, and she wouldn't say no to a new washer and dryer. Maybe it was just human nature to want that which was just out of reach.

Today she was not on the schedule for Pristine Cleaning Service, so she was able to sleep in a little later than usual, and since it was the local school's Christmas break, she was able to spend the day with Stella. If she was counting her blessings, she'd include both those things and add the fact that the sun was out and the temperature above freezing. Today she and Stella would haul the week's laundry down to Lucky's Laundromat, then spend three hours washing, drying, and folding, before they made the trip home again. Although it was tedious, Stella never complained about this particular outing.

Marina sensed that her daughter knew how much this chore aggravated her and upgraded her own behavior and attitude in response. Stella was a joy in this way, a human barometer of other people's emotions, a true people pleaser. It made her an easy child, but it also worried her mother. A little girl who'd lost her father in a car accident shouldn't have to be the one bolstering the remaining parent. She was too young for such an emotional burden. Marina vowed to try harder to stay upbeat around her daughter. It was the least she could do for her.

After stacking their breakfast plates and putting them in the sink, Marina turned to Stella and said, "Guess what we get to do today?" And before her daughter could even answer, she said, "We get to hang out at Lucky's!" She accompanied the declaration with jazz hands, which made Stella laugh. "Clean clothes! It doesn't get any better than that."

Both of them knew the routine. Earlier, Marina had gathered up every quarter in the house, putting the coins into a sandwich bag in her purse. Then she'd collected the week's dirty clothing and threw them into a mesh bag. The towels were due to be washed as well, so she added them to the bag, cramming them in and topping it all with a jug of detergent and a box of dryer sheets.

Together they went out to the garage to get the utility cart. When Ryan had first brought it home, Marina couldn't see a use for it. Now, without a car, she found it came in handy for laundry day and larger grocery store runs.

The walk was short, just a half mile from their house, and the weather was pleasant for December in Wisconsin. Some of the snow was even beginning to melt, making room for future snow-falls. The load in the cart was light. Stella stepped lively, reminding Marina again of her innocence. Someday the world would take that away from her, but for now, it was something to celebrate.

When they got to the laundromat, Stella opened the door for her mother, and Marina wheeled the cart inside. "Go on back by the toys," she told her daughter. "I'll be there in a minute." Marina divided the clothing by color and loaded three machines, adding detergent and coins and starting each load.

She kept an eye on Stella the entire time, watching as her daughter sat cross-legged on the carpeting, entertaining a toddler who was playing with plastic blocks. The little guy's mother was sitting nearby, her gaze locked on an iPad on the table in front of her. When Marina took a seat at the table, the woman looked up long enough to ask, "Is that your daughter?"

"Yes. She's mine. Her name is Stella."

"Stella. What a beautiful name."

"My husband picked out her name." Marina still remembered the look on Ryan's face when the nurse had handed him the baby. Their perfect baby, wrapped in a blanket. The only thing not covered was her sweet face. "Stella Marie," he'd said, tears in his eyes. "She's so beautiful." Sometimes when Stella had an intense look on her face, Marina recognized it as Ryan's thinking face. It was so unfair that he wasn't here to see her grow up.

The woman spoke, interrupting her thoughts. "You should rent her out to babysit here. She's wonderful."

"Thank you. She's a good daughter. I'm very proud of her." Marina could tell that Stella had overheard the praise. She didn't look up, but a slow, wide grin crossed Stella's face.

Stella continued stacking blocks for the little boy to knock down and applauded after each demolition. "Good job!" she said. "You're so smart."

"His name is Dawson," the woman said. "He doesn't say much."

Stella added, "Good boy, Dawson!" And now Dawson, who looked a little confused, began clapping too. On the other side of the laundromat, a machine came to a stop and beeped, and Dawson's mom rose to her feet. "Would you mind watching him for a few minutes while I get my stuff?" she asked Stella.

"No, I don't mind," Stella said.

The woman stuffed her iPad into a backpack, then slung it over one shoulder and went over to the dryers. A few minutes later, having unloaded her laundry, she called out, "I'm just going to run this stuff out to the car. I'll be right back, okay?"

Marina nodded a yes. It always amazed her how casual some people were with their children. This woman had never seen them before and was entrusting her child to them. Of course, neither Marina nor Stella would ever do anything to hurt a child, but Dawson's mother didn't know that. Could it be that Marina was the one who was extreme in that she was overly cautious? Was there such a thing when kids were concerned?

One thing Marina knew—she did worry more than her coworkers. One of the women she cleaned with, Chloe, had three kids who always seemed to be hurting themselves. They played too rough or climbed too high on playground equipment and fell. They always seemed to be scraping their knees or burning themselves while cooking on the stove. On the stove! As if that's what children should be doing. Chloe was fond of saying, "What can you do? Kids will be kids," which seemed lackadaisical, considering everything you could do as a parent to safeguard your children.

But maybe Chloe's way was better. It was possible, Gwen thought, that Chloe's kids would grow up to be bold, independent adults, while Stella would cling to her mother forever. But if this was the end result of keeping her safe, it was a chance Marina was willing to take.

Dawson stood up suddenly and grabbed at the pile of coloring sheets and threw them down on the floor, belly laughing. "You're silly," Stella said, then picked up one of the pieces of paper. "Hey, Dawson! Do you want me to make you something?" She folded one edge to make a square and then proceeded to make fold after fold until she had an origami bird. "See," she said, holding it out to the little boy. "I made you a bird." She waved it through the air. "It can fly."

"Bird?"

"That's right." She handed him the bird, and he regarded it with curiosity.

When Dawson's mom came back from the parking lot, he still had it clutched in his chubby hand. After his mother knelt down to pick up her son, she told Marina, "This was great having your daughter here to entertain him." She laughed. "We should coordinate our schedules so we're here at the same time every week." She leaned over and held out a dollar to Stella. "I'd like you to have this for playing with Dawson. It was sweet of you, and it gave me a nice break."

Stella looked to Marina for approval, and when Marina nodded, she took the money. "Thank you very much," she said. "But I didn't mind playing with him. He's very cute. I like the way he laughs."

Dawson's mom jostled him on her hip. "He does have an adorable laugh." She chucked her son under the chin. "Don't you, you little stinker? Now let's pick everything up so we can go home."

"I can pick it up," Stella said. "I don't mind."

Dawson's mother looked relieved. "Thank you. That's very nice." She directed her attention to her son. "Can you say goodbye to your friend?"

After they'd exchanged their goodbyes and the woman and her son had left the laundromat, Marina asked, "What are you going to do with the money?"

Stella held it out. "I don't really need it, Mama. Why don't you take it for the grocery store?"

What a dear, sweet child. "I have plenty of grocery store money, thank you very much. How about this? Why don't you go over to the vending machine and see if there's a drink you'd like?"

The vending machines had a whole selection of sodas, something they never had at home since the grocery budget was pretty lean. Stella looked over at the machines, and her mother could tell she was deliberating. Finally, she turned to her mom. "Can I have a Dr Pepper?"

Normally, Marina would discourage anything with caffeine, but it was hard to say no when Stella had been so good. Besides, it was early in the day, so it was unlikely to keep her awake tonight. "Only if you let me have a sip."

"I can split it with you."

"I'm not sure I need that much. Just a taste will be enough."

"Okay," Stella said, nodding. "Then that's what I'll get."

8

After folding the clean laundry at Lucky's that day, Marina arranged the clothing and towels into the cart, tucking the bottle of laundry detergent and box of dryer sheets in the side. Sitting on top was the unopened can of soda, which Marina had talked her daughter into waiting to drink until they got home.

"Let's go!" Marina said, mustering her most cheerful voice. In truth, she did feel happier. Now that the laundry was done, the rest of the day was free. Well, except for cleaning the house, but she wasn't going to dwell on that just yet. And maybe some of it could wait. As she got older, dust bothered her less and less.

Stella went ahead and held the outside door open, letting her mother pull the cart out of the building and onto the sidewalk. The cold air hit their faces, but the sun made up for it. Not a bad winter day for a walk.

And after the walk, once they got home, they'd crack open the Dr Pepper. Marina looked forward to having a few moments with Stella at the kitchen table before she put the laundry away. They had so little time together that she tried to make a concerted effort to create some special moments.

After leaving the center of the village, Marina chose to take a slight detour, walking past the nicer part of the community. She loved looking at the historic houses, with their big porches and unique features, especially this time of year when all the houses were decorated for the holidays. Ryan had known all the architectural styles. The homeowners in this area not only had more money, but they also had more time. Nearly every door had a wreath, and the yards were filled with ornate decorations. There was a full-size nativity scene on one lawn. Frosty the Snowman doffing his hat to those passing by. Penguins with necklaces of lights, dancing around a Christmas tree. And her favorite, a complete Christmas village, the houses larger than her microwave.

Must be nice to have that kind of money.

But there she went again, being discontented. She could learn from her own daughter, who wasn't envious of these homeowners. Instead, Stella was delighted just to see the decorations. They paused to admire each yard, Stella pointing out her favorite things. "I love that the Christmas village has a real train!" she said enthusiastically.

They kept walking, and Marina mentally counted her blessings, the biggest of which was walking right next to her, chattering on about the origami swan she'd made for her friend Ivy yesterday. Even though Ivy lived close by, Stella wanted to mail it to her friend inside a Christmas card, to make it a surprise. "Can we mail it to Ivy, Mama?"

"Of course. She's going to love it."

As they made their way down the block, Marina spotted one of Pristine Cleaning's clients, an older woman named Betsy who was on her porch, getting her mail out of the box affixed next to her door. "Hello there," Betsy called out. "Marina, right?"

Marina said, "Yes, that's right. Good to see you, Mrs. Hibbert. This is my daughter, Stella."

Stella waved enthusiastically, and in return, Betsy cupped her hands around her mouth and said, "Nice to meet you."

"Nice seeing you. Have a good day!" Marina said, giving a wave.

When they were out of her sight, Stella asked, "Can I pull the cart now?"

Marina considered the question. It was a sweet offer, but having Stella do it would definitely slow them down. Then again, she had the day off, so what was the hurry? Besides, it was hard to say no to a child who wanted to be of service. She didn't want to discourage her daughter's helping spirit. "That would be lovely, thank you." She gave her the handle. "When you get tired of doing it, we can switch back."

"I won't get tired," Stella promised. "It's easy."

Silently, they continued on. Stella, too busy concentrating on her role piloting the cart, had stopped chattering about Ivy, so Marina found herself with a moment to think about her financial woes. She needed to come up with a way to make more money until her hours at work were restored. She couldn't take on cleaning jobs, as that would conflict with her agreement with Pristine Cleaning, but she did have one idea, which was to post a notice on the grocery store bulletin board offering her services for elder care. Her driver's license was still valid, so she could drive senior citizens to their doctor's appointments or errands, as long as she could use their car. It was possible that Stella could come along as well, eliminating the need for a babysitter. She was a good child, and older people tended to like her. The more Marina thought about it, the more she was convinced that this was actually a promising idea. Knowing that she wasn't completely without options made her feel better.

They paused at a corner, and once Marina looked both ways and indicated it was okay to go, they began to cross the street. Everything was going well until Stella raised one arm to point and cried out, "Mama! Look, it's a dog!"

Marina registered the sight of the animal, a tan-colored dog on the sidewalk on the other side of the street, but she only saw it for a moment, because Stella took off running, still pulling the cart. The dog, sensing her approach, darted into a yard and in a second was out of sight. "Stella, wait!"

Her daughter reached the opposite side of the street first. As she yanked on the handle of the cart to pull it over the cutout in the curb, the rear wheel caught, tipping it over. Almost in slow motion, Marina watched in horror as the contents of the laundry baskets spilled out onto the street.

The towels went down first, landing in a stream of murky slush alongside the curb, and the clothing followed.

"Oh no," Stella said, her face falling. "I'm sorry, Mama. I'm so sorry."

Marina wanted to say it was fine. Not a problem. No worries. She tried to summon the words, but they wouldn't come. Instead, almost out of nowhere, she felt tears come to her eyes. *Darn it!* Why did everything have to be so hard? She blinked back the tears that came anyway, blurring her vision. Finally, she gave in to it, sitting down on the curb and lowering her head into her hands, and the sobbing began. She knew she was upsetting Stella and making a spectacle of herself, but she couldn't seem to help it. What was wrong with her? The last time she'd wept like this was because her husband had died. And now she was having a meltdown over towels?

She felt Stella's arms around her shoulders and heard her voice whispering in her ear. "Don't cry, Mama. I'm sorry. I'll pick it all up." Her daughter's words only made her cry harder.

Marina gulped in some air, trying to collect herself. "You don't have to be sorry, Stella. It was an accident. I think I'm just having a bad week." She reached over and grabbed a washcloth, one that had escaped the puddle, and used it to wipe her eyes. "I'm feeling emotional."

A car passed on the other side of the street, not even slowing down at the sight of laundry in the street while a woman sat on the freezing cold curb crying her eyes out. Marina wasn't looking for sympathy or attention, but still, were people completely heartless? The world, it seemed, didn't care. She was on her own. She patted Stella's hand. "Well, let's get this picked up and keep going."

Together they gathered up the laundry and put it all back in the cart. When they were done, Marina gave her daughter's shoulder an affectionate squeeze. "Well, it's not as bad as I thought. Most of it's still clean."

This time there was no discussion about who would pull the cart. Marina took hold of the handle, and they carried on toward home.

Stella said, "I hope that dog is okay."

"I'm sure it will be fine. It ran into that yard. It probably belongs to those people."

She shook her head. "I don't think so. It looked skinny. And it didn't have a collar. I think it was homeless."

"When we get home, we can check online and see if anyone lost a dog like that. If they did, we can tell them where we spotted it and they can track it down. I'm sure he'll be fine, Stella." She didn't want to sound uncaring, but she only had so much emotion, and today she was using all of it for herself.

"I hope so." Stella didn't sound convinced. "He looked so sad."

wen hadn't slept well that night, her mind whirling with everything going on in her life. Twice she'd fallen asleep only to wake up confused, patting the space next to her. Even after all this time, her subconscious half expected Dean to be beside her. It always took a moment or two to realize he was gone for good.

And then in the morning, as she was simultaneously drinking her coffee and stalking Shawna's Instagram page, her son called. "Hey, Mom!" he said when she answered. He asked how she was doing, just to be polite, and after hearing her obligatory answer came to the real reason for his call. "I hate to do this to you, but some friends are going skiing in Aspen over Christmas and they've asked me to join them. I explained that you and I have plans . . ."

His long pause was her cue. "Don't be silly," she said. "Go. Have fun. We can celebrate when you get back." She managed to sound upbeat, but inside she was dying.

"You don't mind?"

"Of course not. You're young. You should be having fun."

"Thanks, Mom! You're the best."

"I just want you to be happy. I love you, Jared."

"I love you too, Mom."

They continued the conversation for just a few minutes longer, with him promising to call her on Christmas Day. After they hung up, she sobbed.

This was her life now. She was a single homeowner, a retiree with no one to share her time with, and now she would be alone on Christmas. All alone, while all around her people would be celebrating with their families. Making it even worse was the wishing star nagging at her to make a little girl's Christmas wish come true. It was a burden she didn't need.

And it *was* a burden. As long as she held on to the wish, it would weigh on her, make her feel as if she was falling short. She'd listened to Ingrid and was glad to have met Lucky, but really both of them were strangers, with no real insight into her life, so why was she letting them pressure her? They didn't know how precarious her emotional state was right now. She needed to think of her own well-being.

It was at that moment she decided to put the wish back. She dried her tears, then took a long shower, which seemed to help. Once she was ready to face the world, she took one last look at the little girl's wish, put it into her purse, and headed out.

Finding a parking space at the curb in front of the store was a real stroke of luck. As she approached the door, a young man, a plaid scarf peeking out at the neck of his wool coat, held the door open for her. "Thank you!" she said.

"Merry Christmas!" he said with a smile.

Inside, the store was busy and smelled like fresh roasted coffee. The source soon became apparent when she spotted a coffee urn, a pitcher of cider, and a plate of cookies set up on a table toward the front of the store, along with cups, napkins, and a sign that said, *Help Yourself!* Realizing she'd never had breakfast, she poured herself a cup of coffee and took two cookies. They were small.

As Gwen was munching, she heard a woman talking to her son, a little boy who looked to be about kindergarten age. "How many sleeps until Santa comes?" he asked, holding up his two hands, fingers splayed.

His mother counted until she got to the last few digits. "And finally, it's Christmas and Santa comes!"

"Yay!" said the child, his face breaking into a wide grin.

"Today we're buying things for other people. I know it's hard to be patient, but we just have to wait. It helps to think about how happy Grandma and Grandpa will be when they open our gifts. Let's get them something special, okay?" She took his hand, and they walked toward the rear of the store.

Gwen finished the cookies and brushed sugar from the front of her coat. She disposed of her napkin and empty cup in the wastebasket conveniently located under the table. The store was busy today, filled with people milling about. Overhead, she heard piped-in instrumental music playing "Frosty the Snowman." A woman's laughter came from behind one of the bookcases.

She unzipped the front pocket of her purse and pulled out the star, taking one more look. *I wish for a washer and dryer for my mom for Christmas so she doesn't have to go to the laundromat.* Reading it now gave Gwen an uneasy feeling. If she couldn't figure this out, what were the chances someone else could? It was so close to Christmas now that it was unlikely she'd find this child, but she'd already alerted Lucky. Maybe, just maybe, she could solve the mystery before the holiday.

Her intuition told her it was worth a try.

10

The next day, Gwen parked at the curb in front of the house, made her way up the walkway to the front door, then knocked twice. From inside, she heard Betsy call out, "Just a minute."

When the older lady opened the door, her face widened into a delighted grin. "Gwen, how nice to see you! Did you come by for a visit?" She opened the door and ushered her inside. "Such excellent timing. I can introduce you to my neighbor Kayla. She stopped by with her baby just a little bit ago." Betsy beckoned for her to follow, and Gwen found herself walking past a curved staircase and down a hallway until they arrived in the sunny kitchen at the back of the house. A young woman sat with a cloth diaper slung over her shoulder and a tiny baby in her arms. Betsy said, "Kayla, this is Gwen, the one I told you about." She turned to Gwen and said, "Would you like something to drink?"

Before Gwen could answer, Kayla said, "You bought the old Whitfield place, right?" Under the right circumstances, Kayla was probably gorgeous, but today her tired eyes detracted from her good cheekbones and thick hair.

Gwen said, "I wasn't planning on visiting. I'm actually on my way to Lucky's. You mentioned you had some comforters, Betsy? I'd be happy to launder them while mine are being done. I have to sit and wait there anyway, so it won't be any trouble."

"What a nice offer! Let me go get them."

Gwen had thought it would be nice to offer, but somehow she hadn't expected Betsy to take her up on it. *Oh well.* She had the time, and it was a nice thing to do. While she waited, she admired the baby, a little boy with a mist of red hair. "What a cutie. What's his name?"

"Meet Abbott," Kayla said, turning him so Gwen got the full view. "He looks harmless, but he has a voice like an air-raid siren, and he never wants to sleep when I need him to." She continued, telling Gwen how often he'd gotten up the night before. "I'd just fall asleep and he'd start crying again. Longest night ever."

"It's hard, I know." Gwen had vague blurred memories of sleepless nights and exhausted days all running together. She'd watched her son's baby videos recently and had been amazed at how adorable he was. It seemed that Gwen appreciated the baby years more in retrospect than she had at the time. She'd love to go back just for one day so she could fully appreciate it.

Kayla continued. "And then my mother's helper quit because she has some health issues, so I don't even have anyone around to watch him if I need a nap sometimes. I should probably interview a few more people, but I've been too tired to deal with it."

"Can your husband take some vacation time?" Gwen spoke before it occurred to her that Kayla might not have a husband, but from the expression on her face, the question was fine.

"He would if he could," she said. "He took off the first month, and that's all he could do."

Gwen wasn't entirely unsympathetic to Kayla's plight, but she did notice the vast contrast between her own experience and this young woman's. A mother's helper? A husband who took off a month? Back in her day, she'd been her own helper and was lucky if Dean held the baby so she could take a shower. Not all husbands were like that, of course, but judging from conversations with friends, Dean hadn't been alone in this. "It'll get better once he sleeps through the night," Gwen said.

"I hope so," Kayla said with a sigh.

Betsy appeared carrying a large shopping bag, a quilted comforter peeking out of the top. "You sure you don't mind?" she asked, handing the bag over to Gwen.

"Not at all. Happy to do it." Gwen was only telling a small fib. She wasn't really happy at all. The day before she'd felt somewhat better and had vowed not to let her recent divorce get the best of her. But waking up that morning, she'd felt terrible again. Tired and anxious. Sometime while she slept, her spirits had plummeted so much that even getting out of bed was a struggle. Stopping at Betsy's was a way to ward off another wave of grief. She needed something to take her mind off her own troubles, and helping someone else was her solution.

Betsy held out a twenty-dollar bill and apologetically said, "I don't have any quarters, but I think this will cover it."

"I have plenty of quarters. Why don't we settle up later? I can't imagine it will be much."

"Well, if you're sure."

"I'm sure."

After exchanging goodbyes, Gwen carried the bag outside to her car and drove the short distance to the laundromat. The previous night, she had slept soundly. She'd given her brain an assignment to figure out how she could track down a small child with not much to go on. After that, she'd taken a few moments to pray for the little girl and her mother. Her prayers had included the hope that all would go well with them. She'd done some visualizing, imagining a washer and dryer being delivered to their house, an enormous red bow tied around them, just like in the commercials. Gwen didn't exactly believe in Christmas magic, but she wanted to.

She was able to find a parking space right down the block

from Lucky's and managed to carry both her comforter and Betsy's inside in one trip. Only two other people were there, a couple about her age. They sat in adjacent chairs along the wall, apparently waiting for their laundry to finish, but paid no attention to each other. The man's gaze was up at a television, while the woman stared at her phone. The machines for larger loads were entirely vacant, so she was able to stuff the comforters inside two different washers and get things going right away.

When she was done, she took a seat—and almost immediately realized her mistake. She hadn't brought a book or a tablet. She had her phone, of course, but she never found surfing the net on such a small screen entirely satisfying. Looking around, she had the choice of reading a magazine or watching a daytime talk show. Given these options, she settled on a *People* magazine. Even though she didn't know who half the people were, she still enjoyed the read. All the beautiful people in their gorgeous clothes living in their mansions. Their lives a fantasy played out for the public. Who knew what the reality was? It didn't seem to matter.

Gwen was engrossed in a photo collage of women wearing formal gowns at some award show when she became aware of someone standing over her. She looked up to see Lucky, his arms folded, a grin on his face.

"Just the lady I was hoping to see," he said.

"Why is that?" She sat up straight. "Did the girl come in yesterday?"

He shook his head. "I wasn't even here most of yesterday. I had a dentist appointment, and some other stuff came up. But I was thinking about your conundrum the whole time, and last night, I suddenly had a brilliant idea to help figure out who your mystery girl is. Come and I'll show you." He beckoned with one finger.

She set down the magazine and followed him back to the designated children's play area. He strode over to the shelving unit and took out a box the size of a board game, then tilted it so she could see the front.

She read the title aloud: "*The Original Origami Craft Kit.*"

He laughed. "You don't need to sound so enthused." He tapped the top of the box. "Comes with an assortment of papers, an instruction book, and patterns to make all kinds of things. I figured that if your girl or her mom enjoyed origami, they'd be drawn to this."

Gwen nodded thoughtfully. "They would most likely be drawn to this, but so might a lot of other people. Besides, how does this help me find out her identity? I mean, what did you have in mind, that I'd sit here every day and watch for this little girl, then follow her and her mom home when they leave?"

Lucky harrumphed. "That's just part one of my plan. Wait until I tell you the second part—you'll think I'm a genius."

Gwen folded her arms. "Okay, I'm listening."

He leaned in toward her and lowered his voice. "What if I set up a drawing for a free washer and dryer? It would be free to enter —all a person would have to do is fill out a form with their name, address, and phone number."

"So now *you* want to give away a washer and dryer?" she asked, confused. This did not sound like a genius idea to her.

"No. You'll be the one giving it away. Don't you see?" His eyes lit up with excitement. "This is a way for you to give it to her anonymously. I'll set it up like the laundromat is sponsoring it, but you can buy the machines and have them delivered. The little girl's wish will be granted almost like magic."

"So you're going to, what—rig the giveaway? What if you pick the wrong person?" Gwen's mind spun with all the ways this could go wrong. What if Lucky got in trouble for holding an unfair give-away and it led back to her? Was this a crime? Even if it wasn't, how would she go about anonymously paying for a washer and dryer? This was all getting to be too complicated.

"Have a little faith, Gwen." Lucky set the origami kit back on the shelf. "If the heart is willing, a way to grant the wish will present itself."

"I hear you, but I have to say I'm not entirely convinced. I was going to put the wish back on the tree later today if I didn't spot her while I was here."

His eyes widened. "Oh no, don't do that. We're so close to cracking the case."

Now there was a case and he was part of it? "I don't know. What if the mom comes in without her daughter? Or if they start doing laundry at a neighbor's house or something? They might never come here again. So many things could go wrong. And then in the meantime, we're giving away a washer and dryer to the wrong person."

"Look, anything could happen, but I have a good feeling about this. Let me set up the giveaway. I have an empty fishbowl that would work perfectly for the entries. I'll leave the giveaway open-ended so it can go on for weeks if need be, and I won't say how the winner will be chosen, so no one can come back and say it's unfair."

"People will assume it's a random drawing."

He held his palm up. "They can assume what they want. In the meantime, I'll watch for someone who does origami and match the entry they put in the bowl to the mom and daughter that fit your description. Voila! We figured it out."

"Yes, but you're not here all the time. You could easily miss them."

"Huh." He put his fist to his chin. The look on his face showed that this hadn't occurred to him. Not so genius after all.

"Not only that, but everyone who comes in here would probably love to win a washer and dryer. You'll have a lot of entries. There could be multiple mothers and daughters who come in during that time."

"I guess you're right."

"Besides, they'd have to come in between now and Christmas for the timing to be right."

He sighed. "That's true. But would it be the worst thing in the world if they got a new washer and dryer in January?"

"No, it wouldn't be the worst thing, but Christmas is a big deal for kids. I'd hate to see her disappointed," she said.

"I know, but the wish would still be fulfilled. Better than nothing."

They were silent for a minute, both of them mulling over the situation. Finally, Gwen spoke. "You're right. Better late than never. So how about this? What if the entry information has to be written on the origami paper and folded into the shape of a star? You make it a requirement. That will eliminate the people who don't want to be bothered. To make it easier, you can leave the instructions and paper right next to the fishbowl. The star I took off the tree was expertly done, so we'll be able to eliminate any that don't meet that standard. There's a good chance that this will help us narrow it down by a lot."

Lucky smiled. "Brilliant! I have a very good feeling about this. It's only a matter of time."

"We aren't there yet," Gwen said.

"But it's okay with you if I set up the giveaway? If I make the origami star part of the entry requirements?"

Ten minutes earlier Gwen had been ready to tell him to forget the whole thing, but she had to admit that this *might* work. Besides, he had this eager-puppy-dog look that was hard to say no to. They were, apparently, in cahoots together, something that both surprised and amused her. "It's worth a try," she said. "The worst thing that can happen is that I'll give the wrong person a washer and dryer."

"You'd be fulfilling someone else's wish, then, which is still a good thing."

Gwen knew he had a point, but the truth was that she wanted to fulfill a specific wish from this particular little girl. If only there was a way to be sure. "I'll check in periodically to see how it's going," she said.

"Why don't you give me your phone and I'll put my number in your contacts? That way we won't miss each other."

She handed him her phone and watched as Lucky tapped repeatedly at the screen with one curved finger. Handing it back, he said, "Now we're all set." He rubbed his hands together in mock glee. "The game's afoot."

11

On the way home, Gwen stopped in at the grocery store to pick up a carton of coffee creamer. At the last minute, she also decided to grab a bunch of bananas, some peanut butter cookies, and a package of toilet paper. Her arms full, she nearly laughed. How often had it happened that she stopped for one thing and wound up with more? You'd think she'd know to grab a basket on the way in. Well, it served her right. Maybe someday she'd learn.

She had paused to adjust her armload when a young woman pushing a cart stopped, lightly touched her arm, and said, "Just the lady I was hoping to see."

Gwen blinked, not being able to place this person. Making it even more confusing, this woman's opening line was the same one Lucky had used at the laundromat earlier. Gwen knew almost no one in Poplar Creek, and suddenly she was the person two people were hoping to see on the same day. This woman, though, was a complete stranger. Gwen took note of the handbag propped up by the handle of the cart and that the cart contained kombucha, organic blueberries, and goldfish crackers. None of these details helped. "Really?" she said, faking it while racking her brain.

Nothing came to mind. "You wanted to see me?" Clearly, this woman had her confused with someone else.

The woman said, "I'm Laurel. We spoke at the laundromat yesterday? In the kids' area?"

At the mention of the laundromat, a memory came into view, and Gwen suddenly recognized the younger woman as the one who'd been sitting at the table, her toddler son nearby. Today, without the presence of her son, and with her hair pulled off her face, Gwen hadn't initially placed her. The vibrant floral tattoos on her right arm should have given it away, but she'd been too occupied with her armload of groceries to really pay attention. "Of course!" she said, relieved. "You're the one with the cute little boy."

"Dawson," she said with a smile. "He is pretty cute."

"You said you were hoping to see me?"

"Yeah. Weren't you looking for a little girl with dark hair, about eight or nine? You said something about an origami star, I think."

Gwen felt a wellspring of anticipation rise in her chest. *Oh please, let this woman know how I can find the little girl.* "That's right. You have a good memory."

"Right after you left, this mom and her daughter came into Lucky's. The little girl fit your description perfectly. About the right age, dark hair down to her shoulders. She was super sweet, played with Dawson. He totally loved her. I talked to her mom for a little bit. She seemed nice too. This was the first time I've ever seen them."

Afraid to get her hopes up, Gwen asked, "Did you get their names?"

"Not the mom's, but the little girl was named Stella. Isn't that pretty?"

"Very pretty," she said with a nod.

"I didn't think too much of it until I noticed something when I was putting Dawson in his car seat." She unzipped the top of her bag, pulled out a folded piece of paper, and held it out. "Dawson had this in his hand." Gwen did a quick shifting of her armload of groceries before taking the paper from her.

It was an origami bird.

"I remembered what you said about them doing origami. Stella was playing with Dawson, so it's a safe bet she or her mom made this for him. I was in a rush, so I didn't go back into the laundromat. Sorry. I wish I could tell you more, but I thought even knowing her name might be helpful."

"It is helpful. *Very* helpful." Gwen stared down at the slightly crumpled bird. "Stella." She let the name sit in her mouth. A little girl named Stella, kind enough to play with a toddler and whose biggest wish was to ease her mother's workload.

I wish for a washer and dryer for my mom for Christmas so she doesn't have to go to the laundromat.

"I'm so glad we connected," Gwen said. Now all she had to do was ask around and see if anyone knew a little girl named Stella. It wasn't a common name. That would help.

A barrel-chested man came down the aisle toward them, his cart leading the way. "Coming through," he announced, and both women stepped to one side to accommodate him as he bustled past.

"Thank you for letting me know," Gwen said once he was past. "It's a long story and I don't want to get into it right now, but it's important to me that I find her."

"You're welcome," Laurel said. "Glad I could help."

12

After they'd returned home from the laundromat, Marina had posted in multiple places online asking if anyone had lost a dog. She'd given a description of the dog and the cross streets where they'd spotted him. (They kept assuming it was a "he," but it was impossible to know for sure at that distance.) Although a lot of people promised to keep an eye out, no one came forward as the owner. The closest animal shelter was about ten miles away, but still she called them and gave the information. No one had reported a missing dog of that description, but the woman who answered the phone still took notes and jotted down Marina's contact information, just in case.

Over the next two days, Marina went online to check her posts over and over again. While many had left comments showing concern, no one had seen the dog or claimed it. One of her Facebook friends had suggested that it may have been her neighbor's dog, saying, *He often gets loose and makes the rounds.* It seemed likely, but when a picture was posted it was of a smaller dog, chocolate brown with white ears that stood straight up. Clearly not the same one.

Stella was disappointed, of course. "So if the dog doesn't have an owner, does that mean that anyone who finds him can keep him?" Her tone was so wistful, it was clear she hoped they would be the ones who found him and then she'd have a new pet.

If money were no object, Marina would have gladly gotten Stella a dog, even that dog, but money was an object. Already they were hanging on by a thread, so she wasn't about to entertain the idea of paying vet bills and buying dog food. She told her daughter, "Don't be getting any ideas. We can't afford a dog. I'm sorry, but that's just the truth of it." Sometimes it was best to manage expectations ahead of time.

"But if we *could* afford a dog and we found it, could we keep it? Are there rules saying how that works? Is it allowed?"

Marina sighed. "Generally speaking, if no one claims a dog, the person who finds it *can* keep it. But we don't know that the dog was really lost. It might have just gotten loose and returned home already. We're not likely to see it again, Stella. Don't get your hopes up."

"Okay," Stella said, her voice small.

It seemed to Marina that she was often telling her daughter not to get her hopes up, and the thought broke her heart. So many things were out of their reach, but on the bright side, they weren't completely destitute. They were clothed and fed and had a roof over their heads. They also had each other, something an adult could easily appreciate. It was different for kids, though. They only saw what their peers had, and it made them want more.

Marina attempted to soften the blow. "How about this? Tonight after dinner, we'll walk up to Village Square Books and you can use your gift card to get something new. Would you like that?" The gift card had been a birthday present from Marina's parents, and every time they'd been in the vicinity of the bookstore, they remembered that the card was still on Stella's dresser. Marina had offered to put it in her wallet more than once, but Stella hadn't liked that idea.

Stella nodded enthusiastically. "I would love that." The gift card was for twenty dollars, enough to pick out two paperbacks, or one book and some odds and ends. Village Square Books had a nice assortment of bookmarks, reading lights, and greeting cards, and on the counter was a small rack of maple sugar candy, which was always a favorite. In retrospect, Marina was glad they'd forgotten to bring the card with them the last time they'd visited the store.

When she dropped Stella off at Beatrice's house that morning, Stella reminded her, "And tonight we're going to the bookstore, right?"

"Absolutely. You can count on it."

Late that afternoon, when the Pristine Cleaning Service van dropped her off in front of Beatrice's house, she found Stella and Beatrice waiting for her, both of them waving from the front window. After walking home and enjoying a quick dinner of heated-up leftovers, they headed out on foot.

Stella was in a sunny mood, and at the store she spent a long time trying to decide what to buy with her riches. Finally settling on *Grimm House,* a book about a little girl who had to outsmart two witches, she used the rest of her money to buy candy and a booklight so she could read in bed. When she was done, she'd spent just eighteen cents shy of the gift card amount. "Way to use a gift card," the lady clerk said enthusiastically, leaning over the counter to give Stella a high five.

It was times like these that convinced Marina that selling the house and leaving Poplar Creek to move closer to her parents, Stella's grandparents, was not a good idea. Poplar Creek was home. Stella loved her school, her friends, and going to Beatrice's house while her mother worked. Marina's parents were not the nurturing type. She was sure they'd watch Stella in a pinch, but they had their own routines. So she couldn't count on them the way she could Beatrice or even some of her coworkers. Staying in Poplar Creek was an emotional decision, but that didn't mean it was a bad decision.

After paying for the purchase, Marina was ready to go, but Stella said, "Just a minute, Mama. I want to check something. Would you hold my bag?"

Marina took the bag from her outstretched hand. "Of course." Stella was nearly to the tree when she realized what this was all about. She was looking for her wish, the one folded up inside the origami star. With a sinking heart, Marina watched as Stella circled the tree, searching for her wish. After the second time around, she enthusiastically said, "Mama, my wish is gone. Someone took it!"

"Are you sure?" Marina kept her voice on an even keel. "There are a lot of wishes. You may have missed it."

"No. I checked. It's gone."

"It might have fallen off and gotten swept up when the bookstore cleaned the floor."

"I hung it really good so it wouldn't fall off." Stella's eyes lit up with excitement. "I know someone took it. I know it for sure. How long do you think it will take to come true?"

"I don't know," Marina said. "I've heard that sometimes wishes don't get granted." She looked at Stella's excited face and thought about how disappointed she was going to be as time went on without her wish coming true.

"This one will. I think it will happen on Christmas!"

"Maybe, maybe not," Marina said. "I'd give it a few weeks, and if it doesn't happen, you can tell me what the wish is and maybe we can work something out." Stella didn't look like she thought this was a good idea. To provide a distraction, Marina said, "Let's go home so you can start reading that book."

Stella skipped along the way, talking again about the origami swan she'd mailed to her friend Ivy that day. Marina had forgotten all about it, but Beatrice, bless her heart, had gone ahead and taken care of it. It really did take a village. It was cold and pitch-black by now, but they'd dressed for the weather and walked briskly to compensate.

When they approached Mrs. Hibbert's house, the older lady rushed out the front door and waved to get their attention. "Marina!" she said. "I meant to ask you why you're not part of the crew that cleans my house anymore. I missed you yesterday." She was out of breath by the time she joined them on the sidewalk.

"The schedule was changed, and my hours were cut," Marina said. "I should be back in February, though." Betsy Hibbert's house was one of her favorites. One person didn't create much dirt, and the place was always tidy, making it easy to dust and clean counters. Very often, Mrs. Hibbert offered them something to drink and slipped them five dollars each. At Christmastime last year, she'd tipped each of the three of them fifty dollars, something that had endeared her to Marina forever.

Mrs. Hibbert frowned. "I can't say I'm pleased about the change in staffing. That new young woman does a terrible job. I caught her using the same rag to wipe the floor and my kitchen counter." Her nose wrinkled in disgust. "And instead of scrubbing the shower stall, she just spritzed it with glass cleaner and wiped it in like three seconds. Lazy, that's what it is. I was appalled. I gave that boss of yours a call right after the crew left, and she said she'd talk to her."

So Mrs. Krueger's niece wasn't turning out to be a star employee after all. Marina had to fight back a smile. "I'm sorry to hear you had a bad experience."

Mrs. Hibbert frowned. "If they send that girl back again, I'm going to be watching her like a hawk."

This time Marina couldn't hold back a grin. "I understand." Next to her, Stella had pulled her new book out of the bag and was looking at the back cover. Before long, she'd be fidgeting with impatience. She was a good child, but even well-behaved children had their limits.

"But at least you're getting some well-deserved time off," Mrs. Hibbert said. "Are you enjoying your vacation?"

Enjoying her vacation? How did she respond to that? Marina

decided on honesty. "Actually, it's not a vacation, and I'm looking for work to make up for the loss in income. I plan on posting notices for those looking for elder care. I can drive people to appointments, spend time with those who need companionship, that kind of thing. If you know anyone, I would appreciate it if you would give them my information."

Mrs. Hibbert said, "I don't know anyone offhand, but if you give me your contact information now, I'll give it some thought."

Marina, who had come prepared, pulled a printed note card out of her purse and handed it over. "Thank you."

"One more thing."

"Yes?"

"If you and your daughter don't have plans for Christmas Eve, I would love for you to come to my Christmas party. It's an open house, so just drop in anytime after five. It's really fun. Food and drinks, and we sing Christmas carols." She turned to address Stella. "Santa comes and hands out Christmas stockings to the kids, and you can get your picture taken with him if you want."

Stella looked up at her mother. "Can we, Mom?"

"That does sound like fun," Marina said. Mrs. Hibbert meant well, but she was certain Mrs. Krueger, her employer, wouldn't approve of her fraternizing with the customers. She needed the job and wasn't about to do anything to jeopardize her position. And yet, here both Stella and Mrs. Hibbert were looking at her, each with a hopeful expression on her face. She said, "I'm not sure if we'll be able to make it, but thank you for the invitation. I really do appreciate it."

Mrs. Hibbert nodded. "If your plans change, just show up. It would be a nice surprise."

❧ 13 ❧

Against her better judgment, Gwen was now checking Shawna's Instagram page on a daily basis. During a recent phone call with her best friend, Beth had told her, "Just stop looking at it, Gwen. It's a crazy maker. Nothing good can come of it." Beth was right, of course. She always was— not that it made a bit of difference. Gwen vowed to stop checking but caved after only a few hours. She couldn't seem to help herself.

Shawna and Dean were still in Florida, enjoying #beachlife, as free and ecstatic as a couple on their honeymoon. Seeing their happy faces, Gwen normally vacillated between outrage and depression, but on the day Shawna posted a photo of the two of them drinking iced lattes, Gwen noticed something of interest. It was the look on Dean's face, one of thinly veiled tolerance, an expression she knew quite well. It was the face he made when he was trying to appear agreeable, but underneath it all, he'd had enough. When they were together, that expression had always been a signal to her that it was time to leave a dinner party or change the topic of conversation. For more than thirty years she'd deciphered the expressions on this man's face, and she could read him as clearly as if there were a thought bubble printed above his head.

Based on this image, Gwen believed something was troubling him. It could be that he wasn't on board with the iced lattes, something he normally would never have ordered, or that he'd had enough of beach life, or he was tired of having his photo taken for Instagram. Or maybe he just had a headache. It was hard to say from one image. But for the first time, Gwen had the thought that it was possible Dean and Shawna did not have the kind of #foreverlove that Shawna had put out for the world.

The interesting thing was that Gwen wasn't sure how she felt about this. She should be glad, but instead she was conflicted. She'd wanted him to realize he'd made a mistake. On some level, his unhappiness vindicated her. And yet, it wasn't that simple. They had history. She had spent the majority of her adulthood bound to this man, and they had a son together. She'd loved him with all her heart and had showed it in a million ways, large and small. At one time, she'd imagined them together until the very end of their lives. As in, their deathbeds. (In her imaginings he would die first, leaving her a distraught widow.)

And now he was in Clearwater with simple Shawna, possibly regretting leaving his old life, but maybe not. It could be that she was just projecting. Besides, it really didn't matter. Whether or not Dean was happy was not her concern anymore.

She shut off her tablet, put on her winter garb, gathered up her purse, and headed outdoors, locking the door behind her. Today she'd decided to stop in at the laundromat before going to the center of the village. She walked along, enjoying the brisk winter air and the glint of sunlight on the snow. Before she knew it, she had arrived. Pushing the door open and going inside, she was enveloped by a rush of warm air. A half dozen people had arrived before her, all of them busy, doing everything from loading machines to using the money changer to sitting quietly and waiting. She pulled off her gloves and put them in her pockets, then made a beeline to the side counter that held the display for the giveaway. A hand-printed poster showed an illustrated image of a washer and dryer topped by the words, "Lucky's Laundromat Giveaway! Win a washer and dryer. Enter here." The directions were at the bottom. The fishbowl sat in front of the poster, next to the origami instruction book and a stack of folding papers. Fewer people had entered than she would have thought. Maybe half a dozen or so? Presumably, the origami star requirement made it more challenging.

Gwen peered inside the fishbowl, trying to see if any of the entries looked like Stella's star, but it was hard to tell without actually taking them out and inspecting them. When Lucky walked out of the back room and saw her standing there, he gave her a smile. Per usual, he had a comfortable, rumpled look, his face unshaven, his clothing casual, always looking as if he was dressed to chop wood. As always, he appeared happy.

Some people, Gwen realized, were just likeable. Lucky was one of them.

As he joined her in front of the display, she asked, "Any new developments?" During an earlier visit she'd told him the little girl's name was most likely Stella. He didn't know of anyone by that name but had promised to ask around. Gwen had asked her neighbors as well, but so far no one knew a child by that name. And here she'd thought it would be easy. Turned out that even though Poplar Creek was a small village, there were a thousand people.

He shook his head. "No, but I'm not giving up. Most people come in about once a week. If they did their wash a week ago, then they're due any day now. I've been making a point to hang out here more than usual. We'll find her."

"In time to grant the wish before Christmas?" she asked. They had only a few days left for this to work.

He nodded, a gleam in his eye. "If we're lucky, and I usually am."

He sounded so sure. Gwen said, "None of the entries so far are a good fit?"

Lucky shook his head. "No, I've been googling. You'd be amazed what you can find online. I can say for sure that the names on the entries don't fit our girl."

"You're sure?"

"Absolutely. There are five entries in all." He ticked them off on his fingers. "One is a single guy, and three of them are senior citizen couples. The last one is a married woman with teenagers. No younger kids in that family. And no sign of a Stella in the whole bunch."

Gwen glanced back at the fishbowl with its five slightly misshapen origami stars. Behind each star there was someone who desperately wanted to get chosen. Each entry was a wish of its own, the same as if it had been hung on the tree. Little did they know that Lucky was unfolding their pieces of paper, googling their names, and then eliminating them based on what he found. The deception made her feel uncomfortable. These people didn't stand a chance of winning, and yet they probably had some hope that they would, especially given the odds. It was a small consolation that Lucky had set it up. It hadn't been her idea, so why did she feel a twinge of guilt? "I guess we'll just have to wait some more," she said with a sigh.

"Gwen, cheer up. I have a feeling this is going to work out just fine."

"If you say so." Toward the back of the room, an older gentleman whistled as he folded clothes on one of the counters. At least one person didn't mind going to the laundromat.

"I say so," Lucky said. "And as soon as it happens, believe me, you'll be the first call I make."

"And when that happens, we'll go out to lunch to celebrate. My treat," she added.

He nodded. "I'll count on it."

14

Gwen browsed at the bookstore for almost an hour, then took a walk around the downtown before heading back to her house. Lucky's words played over and over in her head. "I'll count on it," was what he'd said in response to her offer to buy him lunch, and it didn't escape her that he'd said it with a charming smile. The topic of her divorce had come up in an earlier conversation, and she knew he was single since he'd said as much. Divorced, widowed, gay? She had no idea, but now it seemed they had a hypothetical date. Nothing romantic, just a date between almost-friends. The idea thrilled her. She'd never imagined she'd be able to make new friends at this stage in her life. It wouldn't have happened, she realized, if Dean was still around. Previously she'd gone through the world as one half of a pair. When you always have a spouse at your elbow, there's not as much room for other people.

The pain at having been discarded by her own husband wasn't going away anytime soon, but she could see that navigating through life alone had opened the door to situations she wouldn't have encountered otherwise. A small silver lining during a very dark period. Maybe there was a light at the end of the tunnel after all.

Turning off the main street, she headed toward the residential section. One block in, she heard something besides the sound of her own footsteps and turned to see a medium-size tan dog, tongue out and panting, trailing her by a few feet. It was cold enough that his breath came out in foggy puffs. Gwen paused and the dog stopped too, looking up at her with dark eyes. She glanced around, looking for his owner. No one was on the sidewalk, and only one other person in the area was outside, a blonde woman wearing a long woolen coat, a knit headband covering her ears. She was coming up the walkway toward the house, an expensive-looking handbag looped over one arm. "Excuse me?" Gwen called out. Once she'd gotten the woman's attention, she pointed and asked, "Is this your dog?"

The woman shielded her forehead with her hand. "No, my dog is in the house."

"Do you know who this one belongs to?"

She shook her head. "Sorry. I've never seen it before."

Before Gwen could ask another question, the woman turned and continued on, signaling the conversation was over. She looked down at the dog, now sitting on his haunches as if waiting for someone. Gwen waved her hand. "Go home, puppy! Go on, home." He didn't budge. She noticed his lack of a collar, but that didn't mean he wasn't someone's pet who had slipped out of the yard. She put her hands on her hips like she'd done when her son, Jared, was being a difficult toddler. "I mean it. Go on home."

The dog didn't budge, and now a small whine came out of his mouth, one that almost sounded like pleading. Gwen looked around the neighborhood, trying to spot his owner nearby. At any moment she expected to hear someone call out and the dog to leave her side, but that didn't happen. She didn't know much about dogs and wasn't sure of the best course of action. Being on foot, she didn't have a car to transport him to an animal shelter, and being new to the community, she didn't even know where there was a facility that took strays. She got out her phone and brought up the Poplar Creek Facebook page, then scrolled through several weeks of posts. Someone had lost and then found a calico cat, but there was nothing posted about a dog. "There has to be someone missing you right now," she said. "You'd better go on home."

He gave a shudder, his ears shaking. If Gwen hadn't known better, she would have thought he was saying no.

"All right, then," she said. "Have it your way, but I'm going home." She continued down the block, aware that the dog was right behind her every step of the way. When she got to the corner, she paused to look both ways, then continued on. She would have bet that the dog wouldn't cross with her, but he did, continuing to shadow her down that block and on to the next one, not letting her out of his sight.

Her theory was that if she didn't acknowledge him, he'd stop trailing her, but her assumption was wrong. The dog kept three feet behind her, no matter what. When she stopped, he halted as well. If Gwen crossed a street, the dog also crossed. When she turned, he turned. This was no coincidence. The dog was doing a better job staying with her than her son had as a preschooler. As a small child, Jared had had a tendency to get sidetracked, but this pup kept a perfect pace and distance behind her.

But why? Had this dog confused her with someone else? Maybe his owner was a lady who looked similar to Gwen? It seemed unlikely. Canines were smart and had an incredible sense of smell. He'd be able to tell the difference between his human and some random woman.

When she was halfway down the next block, she came to Betsy's house. Heading up to the door, the dog following right behind, she gave a few sharp knocks, then waited. Gwen looked down at the dog. "Let's see if Betsy knows who you belong to."

Betsy answered the door with a huge smile. "Gwen, how nice

to see you!" She opened the door and beckoned for her to come inside.

"I really only stopped for a moment," Gwen said. "To see if you know this dog." She pointed to the dog sitting at her side. "He's been following me for blocks now. Do you know him? I'd love to return him to his owner. "

Betsy came out on the porch and reached out her hand for the dog to sniff. "Aren't you a good doggie," she said, cooing. "I like your droopy ears. Yes, I do. You are a sweet thing."

"Have you seen him before?"

Betsy shook her head. "No, and I think I know most of the dogs around here. I have a good memory when it comes to animals." She folded her arms and rubbed them to keep warm. "Come on inside. I'll get him some water and we'll work this out."

Gwen and the dog came inside, then waited on the rug in the entryway as Betsy headed into the kitchen. She regarded the pup, who was now sitting, his head tilted to one side, his eyes right on her. If she didn't know better, she'd think it was a look of devotion. Without even thinking about it, she found herself offering him her closed fist the way Betsy had, and he shimmied forward and bumped his nose against her knuckles. "You're not so bad, are you?" she murmured, and in response he gave her hand a short lick.

Betsy came out then with a bowl of water and a plastic bag the size of an overnight case. She set the metal bowl down at Gwen's feet. As soon as the bowl hit the rug, the dog began to drink. "I knew it," Betsy said triumphantly. "I could tell he was thirsty." They both watched as the dog's pink tongue lapped up water. "This bowl used to be my Zeke's. I had to put him down a few months ago."

"I'm so sorry."

Betsy shook her head. "Only six years old. It broke my heart, but he was in so much pain at the end that I had no choice. Cancer."

"That had to be difficult." Gwen gave her a sympathetic smile.

"It was awful. I cried for days," Betsy said. "You know, it was the craziest thing—for weeks afterward I kept thinking I heard the clinking of his dog tags against his food bowl. Just ever so faintly. Clink, clink, clink. I'd hear it and think it was Zeke and then remember he was gone, and the sound would stop. It's funny how the mind plays tricks on you."

They sat quietly, watching the dog. Finally, Gwen said, "Any suggestions as to how I can get this little guy back where he belongs?"

Betsy shrugged. "Just the usual, I guess. Call the animal shelter and see if someone has reported him missing. Check on Facebook too. There's a Poplar Creek page."

"I already did that. No one reported a missing dog."

"I'd still go ahead and do a post saying you found a dog. Make sure to include a photo. You'll also want to take him to a vet and have him checked out. They'll see if there's a microchip. I recommend Dr. Bach, my old vet. Dr. Boyd Bach. Cool name, right? He's terrific."

Her suggestions sounded involved and time-consuming. "That's more than I had in mind," Gwen said. "Maybe you could take him? Since you're used to dogs?"

"Oh no you don't," Betsy said with a laugh. "He followed you, so he's yours now." She handed Gwen the large plastic bag. "And to help you out, here are some of Zeke's things."

Gwen wanted to push the bag away, but something made her take it instead. When she peered inside, she saw an unopened bag of dry dog food, a pouch of dog treats, shampoo, a food dish, and a collar and leash.

Betsy added, "For some reason, I just couldn't get rid of these things. Now I know why. They were meant for you."

Meant for Gwen? That sounded a little woo-woo, but she supposed Betsy meant well enough. Still, Gwen had no intention of taking Zeke's things. She held out the bag. "I think you should keep this. I can take this little guy to the animal shelter. I've never had a dog and wouldn't even know what to do with him. They'll be equipped to take care of him." As if the dog understood he was the topic of conversation, he stopped drinking to watch them.

"Sorry. He's yours now," Betsy said, shaking her head. "If you're taking him to the animal shelter, you can take those things along with you and donate them. I checked—the food hasn't expired, so they can still use it." Betsy reached over and patted the dog's head. "Good boy, yes you are. You can tell them he's a mixed breed. Medium-size, maybe thirty-five pounds or so?"

More and more it sounded to Gwen like Betsy was the one who should take him. "Where is the animal shelter?"

"Closest one is about ten miles away. I have to tell you, though, that it's not a no-kill shelter."

Not a no-kill shelter. Gwen had to think about the double negative for a second before she realized that it meant this shelter did euthanize animals. Certainly, it wasn't commonly done? She would have guessed that it was a last resort, only opted for in the case of vicious or terminally ill animals. This dog, although a little on the thin side, was clearly good natured and healthy.

While Betsy was talking, the dog came over to Gwen and rested his head against her knee. She leaned over to stroke his head and scratch behind his ears. "Don't you worry," she said. "We'll find your owner."

Betsy grinned. "I think he already did."

15

Before they left, Betsy put the collar and leash on the dog, and he stood politely while she did so. "What a good dog," she cooed. She gave Gwen instructions for taking care of the dog, including giving out the food in small amounts. "If he's overly hungry, he might overeat and puke. I had a dog who did that once. Poor thing. Once we started to parcel it out, it took care of the problem." She had so many suggestions that Gwen could have taken notes, but all of it seemed pretty straightforward. Gwen listened politely, knowing that she didn't have to commit this to memory because the dog was not staying with her.

No. Not going to happen.

She'd never had a dog, and she wasn't about to get one at age fifty-nine. She knew from friends that it was harder to travel when you had a dog. You had to have a friend or family member willing to take the dog, or you had to pay a boarder, and everyone knew the good ones charged an arm and a leg. She and Dean had taken a trip with another couple, and the wife had spent a good part of the time texting the boarder (Puppy Paradise, if she remembered correctly) to check on their dog, Norman. She'd been worried about Norman thinking they'd abandoned him.

Eventually, the boarder sent a video clip of Norman playing with some of the other dogs, having the time of his life, which calmed her fears somewhat. To Gwen, having a dog was too much like having a child. She was through with all that.

She'd let Betsy put the collar and leash on the dog, but if it were up to Gwen, she would have left the collar off. What if the real owner saw her walking their dog? She'd look like a dog-napper. Besides, she didn't want to force the dog to come with her. Secretly she hoped he would fight her on this, opting to stay with Betsy, which would relieve her of the responsibility.

No such luck.

The dog trotted alongside her as if they'd done this a hundred times before. He didn't strain at the leash or cross her path. This was a well-behaved dog. Someone had to be looking for him.

At the end of the block, Gwen saw Betsy's neighbor Kayla pushing a stroller with a blanket covering the front. Gwen asked if she knew of anyone who'd lost a dog, or if she'd seen that particular dog before, but Kayla just shook her head, abruptly saying, "Sorry, no," before turning onto what Gwen assumed was her own driveway.

Gwen wasn't offended. Everyone knew that new mothers were usually short on sleep. When everything was an effort, life had to be prioritized, and helping find lost dogs' owners was not high on the list.

When they arrived at her house, the dog followed her inside. Gwen set down her purse and got to work, unsnapping the leash and putting the dog's food and water bowls in the corner of the kitchen, then filling each, being careful not to put too much kibble in the food dish. When the dog started eating, Gwen got out her tablet. "You let me know when you have to go out, okay?" she said. "No peeing in the house."

Once her device was powered up, she looked up the name and phone number of the animal shelter. Just as Betsy had said, it was about ten miles away. On the website they didn't say anything about their policies regarding euthanizing pets but had a general statement that implied as much: *We have an open-door policy and will take all animals, but we reserve the right to make health and life decisions regarding the animals in our care. Adoptable pets are given top priority.*

Gwen frowned, then addressed the dog. "I can't say I approve of their way of doing things." Shaking her head, she took a seat at her kitchen table, then got out her phone and called the shelter.

After she gave her name and described the dog, the woman on the other end of the line said, "This is sounding familiar. I think someone did call about a medium-size dog with a light brown coat. Mixed breed, right?"

"I think so."

"Just a sec. Let me look."

Gwen reached down and gave the dog's head a good rub. "You are a good boy, aren't you?" Without intending to, she'd adopted Betsy's cutesy tone. It didn't take much. He *was* a good boy, sweet and well behaved. He leaned into her hand as she petted his head, so she kept going. When the woman came back on the line, her voice startled Gwen.

"Thanks for waiting," she said. "Someone did call about a dog fitting that description, but it was just a notification of a loose dog in Poplar Creek, so I guess that's what I was thinking of."

"I'm calling from Poplar Creek, which is where I found him." Gwen lowered her head to meet the dog's eyes. "I bet it's the same dog."

"Most likely."

"So if I bring him in, do you have space for him?"

"Sure."

The response was decidedly lackluster. Gwen tried again, "I assume he'll get medical care and you'll try to find his owner?"

"Sure." The woman's voice was accompanied by the sound of papers being shuffled.

Again, not very reassuring. "I'm sorry for belaboring the issue, but this dog is really a sweetheart. I'd like to be certain that he'll get the best possible care and that if no one comes forward, you'll find him a good home."

The paper shuffling stopped. "You sound like you've grown fond of this dog."

"Not necessarily. I mean, I just found him today." She'd stopped petting him, so he pressed his nose against her thigh. When her fingers found the back of his ears, his tail began to thump against the floor.

"And yet you want guarantees that he'll have a happily ever after." She sighed.

"It certainly would be reassuring to know he'll be fine. Could I maybe get some updates on how he's doing? If I call, would someone tell me?"

"I'm going to tell you what I tell everyone who's conflicted about relinquishing an animal. The only way you can be guaranteed of a positive outcome is if you keep the animal. Once you hand him over to us, we reserve the right to make health and life decisions regarding that animal. I'm sorry to tell you our staff is stretched pretty thin, so giving out updates is not something we do."

"I see." So if she dropped him off at the shelter, she'd never know what happened to the little guy.

"Why don't you just keep him?" The woman's voice had softened. "You can take him to a vet and get him scanned for a microchip, or we can do it here for you. We'll keep his information on file in case the owners come forward, but since no one has called so far, it's a good guess that he's on his own."

"But he had to come from somewhere," Gwen said. "When I walked him on a leash, he heeled. He's a little gentleman. Someone had to have trained him. Why would they suddenly not have him?"

"I don't know what to tell you," the woman said. "I don't understand it either, but some people just change their minds about having a pet. They move and the new place doesn't allow animals, or they have a baby, or the new girlfriend doesn't like the dog, or someone becomes allergic. We've heard all kinds of reasons."

"That's just heartbreaking."

"I agree." After a pause, she said, "So you're keeping him, then?"

Gwen lowered her gaze and met the dog's big brown eyes. "I guess. For now. I'll take him to a vet and get him scanned for a microchip. Then I'll see what happens after that."

"Sounds good. Why don't you go ahead and email me a photo of the dog, along with your contact information? The email address is on our website."

"I will," Gwen promised.

"And after you get the dog scanned for a microchip, you can update us."

"Will do."

"All right, then. If we can help, just give us a call. Good luck."

The phone line clicked before she was even able to say goodbye.

16

That night, Marina was awakened by the softest of sounds coming from across the hall. She sat up and listened, her mother's instincts on high alert. Nothing. Whatever had made the noise had stopped, and all was quiet now. Even so, she knew she wouldn't be able to fall back asleep until she'd checked on Stella.

Throwing back the covers, she got out of bed, stopping to put on her slippers before walking to the door. A nightlight in the hallway showed Stella's bedroom door, slightly ajar, as it always was at night. Quietly, she gave the door a gentle push and saw her daughter, not in bed, but instead kneeling on the bench in front of her window. The blinds were up and the window sash raised. A cold draft wafted into the room. "Stella? What's going on?"

Stella turned. "Mama," she whispered. "I think I saw a shooting star."

"It's the middle of the night." She crossed the room and knelt next to her daughter. "And it's way too cold to have the window open." She pulled the window down and secured the latch.

"It was just for a minute." Stella pressed her hand against the glass. "I was trying to see better. Ivy told me if you wish upon a shooting star your wish will absolutely come true." She turned, and even in the dim light Marina saw the gleam in her eyes. "And I think I saw one. One of the stars moved!"

Again with the wishing, and now Ivy was contributing to her daughter's delightful delusions. Marina pulled down the blinds and turned to Stella. It was time for the truth. "She did, huh? I've heard that before, but I'm sorry to tell you that it's not true. Sometimes wishes don't come true at all, sweetie." She stroked her daughter's hair. "But if you tell me what you're wishing for, we can talk it over. Maybe I can help."

"I told you before, Mama, I can't tell you. It's a surprise."

"Wait a minute. Is this the same wish you put on the tree at the bookstore?"

She nodded. "The same one. It's such a good wish. Sometimes when I'm in bed at night and I'm thinking about how much I want it to come true, I feel like it's already starting to happen. Like magic."

Marina had a sudden sinking feeling. "Stella, if you're wishing that your dad would still be alive, that's not going to happen."

Stella quickly said, "I know that."

But did she? "Okay, just so you understand that."

"I'm not a baby. I know that when someone dies they don't come back."

Marina nodded. "You should be sleeping. Let's get you tucked into bed," she said, guiding Stella away from the window. As her daughter slipped under the covers, Marina made a point to tuck the blankets around her. "Now you're all cozy." She kissed her forehead. "See you in the morning."

"See you in the morning," Stella repeated softly. "Mama?"

"Yes?"

"I know you don't believe me, but you'll see. When the wish comes true, you'll be so happy."

"I'm already happy because I have you as a daughter." She went to the door and looked back, reassured to see Stella tucked under the covers, safely in bed. "Sweet dreams."

17

D ecember 23

GWEN SAT IN THE TINY WAITING ROOM OF VETERINARIAN DR. Boyd Bach, the dog curled up at her feet. She had him on the leash, not that it was necessary. This little guy was content to stay right by her side. More loyal than her husband had been at the end of their marriage, she thought with a wry grin.

When they'd checked in at the garland-strung front desk, the receptionist, a lady named Donna, had told her the doctor was about fifteen minutes behind schedule. "Not a problem," Gwen had assured her. "We've got time." And she did have time, which was not the same thing as having nothing to do. Lately, between trying to track down the wishing girl and dealing with the dog, she'd been busy and too preoccupied to dwell on herself. She hadn't felt lonely since the day the mail lady had knocked on her door to check on her, and she hoped this new state of mind would continue.

The dog rested his head on her booted foot, and she smiled, thinking about the trust it took for him to plant himself that way. Someone had lost a really great dog.

When the outer door opened, she glanced up to see someone she knew, a woman carrying a small pet carrier. She walked right past Gwen and straight to the counter. "Ingrid Gallagher, here with Whiskers." Donna checked her in and cheerfully said, "Dr. Bach is a little behind schedule, but if you'll take a seat he'll be with you as soon as possible."

As she seated herself, a flash of recognition crossed Ingrid's face. "Gwen, how nice to see you!" In the cat carrier on the seat next to her, Whiskers let out a sad-sounding meow. Ingrid leaned over and peered through the grate. "It's okay, baby. Just hang in there."

"Hi, Ingrid. It's good to see you too."

Looking up, Ingrid noticed the dog at Gwen's feet. "I had no idea you had a dog!" Her face broke into a grin. "What a cutie."

"He's not mine," Gwen said hurriedly. "I'm just having him checked out."

"For a friend?"

"No," Gwen said, pausing to think of how to explain things. "It's kind of a funny story. This dog just followed me home one day. For blocks and blocks, actually, right by my side. I've been asking around looking for his owner, but no luck so far. By any chance, do you know anyone who lost a dog?"

A slow smile stretched across Ingrid's face. "No, but I know a dog who *found* someone. And how often does that happen?" She put a protective arm over the cat carrier. "Looks like the universe is sending you all kinds of gifts lately. A wish to be granted and a loyal dog. You have an enviable life, my friend." Ingrid was nothing if not consistent.

"I'm not so sure about that," Gwen said. "I'm certain someone is looking for this little guy. He's really a sweetheart. I wouldn't want to keep him from his rightful owner."

Ingrid nodded. "You have a wonderful outlook, but if there's no owner to be found, I think you should give him a chance. He looks like he deserves one."

"Certainly someone needs to give him a chance."

Gwen was relieved when Donna popped her head up from behind the counter and said, "Gwen Hayward, Dr. Bach is ready to see you."

"Nice talking with you, Ingrid." She stood, and the dog did too, enthusiastically rising to his feet. Donna led them down a short hallway and into an examination room. A moment later, they were joined by Dr. Bach, a whip-thin man with silver hair, wire-rim glasses, and a calming voice that reminded her of Mister Rogers. After he introduced himself to Gwen, he turned his entire attention to the dog. "So this is the mystery pup," he said, giving the dog a head rub. "What is your story, little man?" He gave Gwen a reassuring nod. "We'll see what we can find." He went to a cabinet on the far side of the room and pulled out a white instrument the size of a windshield ice scraper. "A microchip scanner," he explained.

Going back to the dog, he unfastened the leash and crouched down next to him. "You're a good boy. Let's see if we can find out more about you." He began over the dog's head, then scanned his back on both sides, finally doing his legs. When he was through, he met Gwen's eyes. "No microchip, I'm sorry to say." He lifted the dog onto the table and gave him a complete examination, weighing him, taking his temperature, checking every part of his body, and listening to his heart and lungs with a stethoscope. All the while, Gwen watched from her seat on a plastic chair against the wall. After finishing the exam, the vet asked, "Did you bring in a fecal sample?"

"Me? No. I didn't know I was supposed to. I mean, I thought if a microchip could identify him that he'd be going back to his owner."

"Hmm." Dr. Bach had a thoughtful expression. "Weren't you

the one who told Donna that you'd already posted on Facebook and checked with the animal shelter and no one reported the dog missing?"

She had mentioned it when she'd made the appointment, but she was surprised that he knew. "That's right. I did tell her that."

"Looks to me like you've got yourself a dog." He grinned.

"Oh no," she said. "I wasn't planning on keeping him."

"You can't afford the expense?"

"It's not the money. I've just never had a dog before."

"Is he a behavior problem? Because I can recommend an excellent dog trainer."

"Actually, he's very well behaved," she admitted. "It's just that I've been going through a lot of changes lately, and I wasn't planning on getting a dog."

Dr. Bach lifted the dog off the table and set him gently on the floor. The dog went straight to Gwen, nuzzling her knee. "He seems to have claimed you."

"I was thinking that he might find a more suitable home at the animal shelter. I'm sure some family looking for a well-behaved dog would love him."

"Maybe so. That's assuming he gets adopted." With one finger he pushed his glasses up his nose. "I've heard some people say they're not real impressed with that facility. Don't quote me on that, though, because I'll deny I said as much."

Gwen could read between the lines. She'd seen enough sad puppy commercials on TV to get a mental image. "Are you saying I shouldn't take him there?"

"I'm saying that this is a good dog, and you might want to consider trying each other out." He reached down and gave the dog another head rub. "At least through the holidays. He's unlikely to be adopted in the next few days." He lowered his head to line up with the dog's. "You deserve a good Christmas too, don't you, boy? Yes, you do."

"Maybe you should take him," Gwen said.

Dr. Bach laughed. "Are you kidding? I already have two dogs and three cats. My wife would kill me. No, he's much better off with you. Just give him a chance."

A chance? Didn't everyone deserve one? The dog rested his nose on her knee. She glanced down to see big brown eyes staring up at her. Adoringly. "Okay, I'll keep him," she said. "At least for now."

"You can drop off that fecal sample anytime," he said. "Oh, and he needs a name too."

Gwen nodded. "Funny you should mention it, because just this minute I decided on a name. I'm going to call him Chance."

18

D*ecember 24*

By the next morning, despite her best efforts, Chance had claimed a spot in her heart. Using the shampoo Betsy had given her, she'd given him a bath the night before, and he'd let her lather and rinse his coat without objection. When she lifted him out of the tub and set him on the floor, the dog shook vigorously, giving her a shower of her own. Shocked, she jolted backward, then laughed and used the towel in her hand to dab her own face before spreading it out on Chance's back. As she gave him a good rub, she realized that the sound of her own laughter was something she'd been missing lately.

After his coat dried, she arranged some blankets on the floor next to her bed and led him to the spot to indicate that was where he should sleep. Gwen was relieved when he curled up in the middle of the blankets. "Tomorrow we'll get you a dog bed," she said. There was still a possibility someone could claim him, but now it seemed less likely, and with every passing minute he was becoming more and more hers.

As usual, she'd woken in the middle of the night and reached out across the bed, only to find Chance curled up beside her. Gwen had given him a gentle pat, then easily sank back into sleep.

In the morning, he crunched on his dog food while she ate breakfast. When she came out of the shower, Chance was sitting outside the door, patiently waiting. By the time she'd gotten dressed and was ready for the day, she was used to having a shadow. "Anyone would think we've been together for years," she said, giving him a pat.

Leaving him behind was unthinkable. She had no idea what he'd do when left alone, and besides, it seemed easier just to bring him along.

She texted Lucky: *Coming by the laundromat to check on the entries. Okay if I bring my dog?*

He answered: *Any friend of yours is a friend of mine!*

It made her smile.

When she walked into the business, Chance on the leash, Lucky was waiting for her, leaning back against one of the counters, a slow grin crossing his face as she came through the door. Instrumental Christmas music played throughout the laundromat, and she smiled as she mentally inserted the lyrics: *Pa rum pum pum pum.*

"Thanks for letting me bring him," she said, holding up the leash.

Lucky leaned over and offered to let Chance sniff his knuckles. "Of course. We're very pet friendly here." He met her eyes. "I didn't even know you had a dog. What's his name?"

"I'm calling him Chance, but I just got him. He followed me home the other day, and I haven't been able to find his owner."

"Did you try . . ."

"I posted it on the Poplar Creek Facebook page, checked with the animal shelter, and took him to the vet. No microchip."

"Sounds like you got it covered." Lucky nodded in approval. After a pause, he said, "My ex-wife got our dog in the divorce. That was a heartbreaker."

"I didn't know you were divorced."

"Yep." He pushed up the brim of his baseball cap. "It was a long time ago. My daughter was a sophomore in high school, and now she's twenty-five. It wasn't a great marriage, but it was still rough when it ended."

"I'm sorry."

"Don't be. I'm good now." He took off his cap and ran his fingers over his hair. "Anyway, on to business. Why don't we go back to my office so we can talk?"

A glimmer of excitement stirred in Gwen's heart. Going somewhere private could only mean that he'd found her mystery girl. It was the day before Christmas, so they were cutting it close. Too close, really. There wasn't time to give an actual washer and dryer to someone, but Gwen could still give the promise of the two appliances to the little girl via a gift certificate. The important thing was that the child would know her Christmas wish had come true. She and Chance followed Lucky to the back of the laundromat, passing a young couple who looked to be in their early twenties. The young woman sat on the counter talking, while the guy folded towels, an amused look on his face. In the back, a woman sat at the table in the kids' area while two boys played with blocks on the rug.

When they entered his office, Lucky closed the door behind them and gestured for her to take a seat opposite his desk. Gwen noticed a framed photo of a ship on the wall behind his desk and a milk crate filled with books. She sat down and Chance sat next to her. "So what's the good word?" she asked.

He raised his eyebrows as he took a seat. "The good word?"

"I assume you found her. Tell me all about it." Gwen settled back in her chair, waiting for the story to unfold.

His face fell. "I'm sorry, but I didn't find her. We've had three more entries, but none of them are a match."

"Oh." Gwen felt her disappointment wash over her. "So now what? I give the washer and dryer to someone else? Or do we wait a few weeks?"

Lucky sighed. "This is what I'm thinking—we wait a few weeks, and if we don't find the girl, I'll give away the washer and dryer to a different winner. It was my idea to make it a contest, so you shouldn't have to pay for it. I'll do a random drawing to make it fair."

"We can split the cost," Gwen said. "I'll still be doing a good deed, just not the one I intended to do."

"I know it's a letdown. I really thought it would work," he said with a shake of his head. "I just don't know what else to do."

"I think it's just a matter of timing." Gwen reached down and absentmindedly gave Chance a pet. "I have a thought—what if we go to the elementary school and ask if they have a student named Stella? Don't you think they'd tell us if we explain the reason why?"

"I don't know," he said, shaking his head. "In this day and age, you can't just wander into an elementary school and ask them for information about one of their students. I think it would come off as creepy. And maybe illegal."

"You don't know anyone who works at the school?"

"No." He shook his head. "The only teachers I know are retired." He suddenly brightened and held up one finger. "But my sister, Ingrid, might know of someone from the school! I swear she knows everyone."

"Ingrid from the bed-and-breakfast is your sister?" she asked in amazement.

"That's right." He tilted his head and gave her a long look. "Why do you sound so surprised?"

"I don't know. I just wouldn't have guessed," she said, hoping she hadn't offended him. Lucky came off as being down-to-earth, while Ingrid seemed to exist on another dimension. "You don't look alike. Also, she seems very . . . different."

"That's my big sister," he said, shaking his head. "You have to love her. I know she seems a bit out there, but it's amazing how many times she's right. I find myself asking her advice all the time."

"She is good at giving advice," Gwen admitted.

"Which reminds me—Betsy Hibbert told me you're invited to her party tonight. Are you planning on going?"

"Oh, I don't know." She glanced down at Chance. "I'm not sure what I'd do with Chance. I've never left him alone, and I don't have a crate. This is all so new . . ."

"Bring him along," Lucky said. "He'll fit right in."

"I'd love to go, but I'm not sure Betsy would appreciate me bringing a dog."

"Let's find out."

He pulled out his phone, and even as Gwen was saying, "You don't have to do that," he'd already initiated the call, which he put on speakerphone.

After Betsy answered, he said, "Hey, Betsy, Ben Gallagher here. I'm with Gwen and her new dog. Do you mind if she brings the little guy to your party tonight?"

"She decided to keep him?" The delight in Betsy's voice rang through. "Such good news! Yes, tell her to please bring her dog to the party. I'd love to see him again!"

Gwen leaned forward. "Hi, Betsy!"

"Hi, Gwen, can't wait to see you tonight. And, Ben, I hope you're bringing your famous apple bread."

"You know it!" he said. "It's baked, sliced, and ready to go. I'll drop it off later this afternoon so you'll have it ahead of time." They wrapped up the call, and when it was over, Lucky turned to Gwen and said, "Problem solved."

"You have famous apple bread?"

"I do. Wait until you taste it. You'll have a whole new appreciation for my talents." He gave her a flirtatious smile.

"Do you prefer to be called Ben or Lucky?"

"I go by either," he said. "Betsy was my daughter's third grade teacher, so she knows me as Ben, but you can call me whatever you want." He tapped his fingers on the desk. "So, now that you're going to the party, how about we go together. Make it a date?"

A date. She hadn't gone on a date in decades and hadn't thought she ever would again. The idea gave her a thrill. "I'd like that. You know where I live? The old Whitfield place?"

He nodded. "I know the place. I'll be there at six. With bells on."

With bells on. An old-fashioned expression, one her grandfather had used. Perfect for Christmas Eve. "Sounds perfect."

19

Marina didn't realize the oven was broken until she'd already seasoned the raw chicken for that night's dinner. She kept entering the temperature on the digital display and pushing Start, but no matter how many times she did it, the thing refused to accept the numbers. She tried pushing the button for the warming oven setting, but that didn't work either. She stared at the heating element, unsuccessfully willing it to work.

Dead. The oven was completely useless.

She wondered how much it would cost to fix or, worse yet, to replace the oven. It didn't matter if it was just ten dollars—it was money she didn't have. She tried to look on the bright side. They still had a microwave, and she could make sandwiches, but this was small consolation. The malfunctioning oven was not her only problem. Stella had not stopped talking about her Christmas wish, and Marina was almost certain her daughter would be disappointed with what she found under the tree the next morning. This was shaping up to be a terrible Christmas, one filled with letdowns and heartbreak. Tears welled up in her eyes.

Stella wandered into the room. "How much longer till dinner, Mama? I'm starving."

"You're not starving, Stella!" She opened the oven door and repeatedly slammed it shut, then went into the other room and lay down on the couch, not even trying to keep from crying. She sobbed into the cushions until she felt a small hand on her head, stroking her hair.

"I'm sorry, Mama."

Marina sat up. "No, I'm sorry, Stella. I'm having a bad day, and I took it out on you. I shouldn't have done that." She pulled her daughter into a hug. Sometimes she wished Stella was still small enough to pull onto her lap. When had she outgrown that? If Marina had known it would be the last time, she would have cherished it more. "The oven is broken, so I can't make the chicken, and I was really frustrated and upset. Everything has been going wrong lately, but it has nothing to do with you."

Stella's voice was quiet. "We don't have to have chicken."

"You're right. How about a bowl of cereal for dinner?"

Later, as they sat at the table eating cold cereal, Stella again brought up the Christmas wish. "You're going to be so excited, Mama. Just wait and see."

Marina looked at her sweet, innocent face and didn't think she could bear a Christmas morning disappointment. Better for her to know the truth now. "I have to be honest with you, Stella. The Christmas wish that you wrote on your origami star is not going to come true. I'm not trying to make you sad, but I know this for certain. You aren't going to get that wish, but you will get other gifts, and I hope you enjoy them." She looked down at her bowl of cereal and scooped up a chunk of banana with her spoon.

"It's not going to come true?" Stella's face scrunched in confusion. "How do you know?"

For the first time in her life, Marina lied to her daughter. "I found out that one of the people who work at the bookstore accidentally threw your wish away. They didn't understand that there was a wish inside. I'm sorry."

Seeing her daughter's sad face made her immediately regret the dishonesty, but it was done. And at least she would be prepared tomorrow.

"They shouldn't have thrown it away," Stella said quietly.

"I know. It was a mistake. People make mistakes."

"It was the best wish too." Her lower lip trembled. "And I wanted it so bad."

"I know." Was there anything worse than not being able to shield your child from the sorrows of life? Marina knew that eventually Stella would have greater problems than an unfulfilled wish, but that didn't matter right now. At the moment, her disappointment was keen, and Marina felt it as well, the way mothers do. Suddenly, a thought came to her. "I have an idea. Why don't we go to Mrs. Hibbert's Christmas party? She said they would be singing carols and Santa would be giving out Christmas stockings to the kids. I'm guessing there'll be some good food too. What do you say?"

A smile crossed Stella's face. She set down her spoon. "I say yes!"

Gwen changed clothes for the party, picking out a red top, gray pants, and black boots. Rummaging around in her jewelry box, she found a novelty necklace made up of fake Christmas tree bulbs, which she paired with silver earrings. After that, she double-checked her makeup, gave her hair a fluff, and surveyed the results in the bathroom mirror. Not too shabby. Her friend Grace had once proclaimed, "I'm not going to get any younger or thinner, so I might as well make peace with how I look," and that had stuck with her. Looking at her reflection, she had a newfound appreciation for her friend's wisdom.

At 5:58, she got her winter coat on and snapped the leash onto Chance's collar. He perked up and began prancing around, anticipating the excitement of a walk. "Sorry, boy," she said. "Not a walk, but we are going somewhere." As they waited on the front porch, the dog was clearly eager to go, but admirably he held back. When she told him to sit, he did so immediately. "Good boy!" She reached down to give him a head rub, and he tilted his head so she'd get the right spot. What a smart dog.

The temperature had dropped considerably, and now in the

crisp night air, she could see her breath and Chance's too. It would be good to climb into a heated car.

Earlier, she'd stuck her phone in her coat pocket, close at hand in case Lucky texted or called to say he was delayed, and now, out of habit, she pulled it out. She was in the middle of checking her messages when she heard the jingle of bells off in the distance. Chance heard it too, his gaze moving in the direction of the sound, now getting louder and accompanied by the rhythmic clip-clop of horses' hooves. She led the dog off the porch and went down the front walkway to the sidewalk to get a better view. Her mouth dropped open when a horse-drawn wagon outlined with Christmas lights turned the corner at the end of the block and headed in her direction. Even more astonishing, Santa was the driver. When he was almost to Gwen's house, he called out, "Whoa, boys!" and pulled back on the reins, coming to a halt right in front of where she stood. At close range, she saw that the wagon had panels on each side that made it look like a sleigh. Bells decorated the horses' harnesses, and inside, the wagon had two rows of seats. Santa, who looked down from the front seat, had a very familiar smile.

Up and down the street, doors flew open and neighbors came out to see what was going on. A little boy down the street yelled, "Hi, Santa!" and Lucky waved back and called out, "Merry Christmas!"

He hopped down off the sleigh and held out his hand. "Your chariot awaits, milady."

With a grin, she allowed Lucky to help her up to the front seat. Chance leaped up to join her, and she got him settled on the seat next to her. As he handed her a red velour lap blanket, she said, "This isn't what I expected when you said you'd pick me up at six." She arranged the blanket across her lap and tried to cover Chance as well, but the dog was having none of it.

"Why, am I late?" Even behind the fake beard his smirk came through. "Or is it that you never imagined dating Santa?"

"It's the second one."

"Fair enough." With a flick of his wrists, he gave the reins a good shake, setting the two horses in motion. "But I did say I'd be here with bells on."

"That you did. You're an interesting man, Lucky Gallagher." The more she learned about Lucky, the better she liked him. "So, were you planning on being Santa tonight, or was this a last-minute idea?"

"I've been the Santa at Betsy Hibbert's party for going on ten years. I also try to make it to some nursing homes and do a few other visits during the season. Just for fun." He glanced over to her. "It's the best part of my year, if you want to know the truth."

He made an impressive Santa. The beard and white hair looked so real, it could have been his own. The outfit looked authentic. The red jacket and pants were made of thick velour and covered what had to be a good amount of padding. The white fur edging of the suit and hat looked soft to the touch. His black boots were shiny, as was the wide belt. "So where do you keep the horse and wagon the rest of the year?" she asked, speaking loudly over the sound of the horses and the jangling of the bells.

Lucky laughed. "They belong to a friend of mine, Trent. He's going to meet me at Betsy's and hold on to them until I need to leave the party. Betsy already has the stockings I give out to the kids. We're a well-oiled machine."

"The children don't ask why you don't have a sleigh and reindeer?" she wondered aloud.

"Oh, they do. You can't get anything past kids nowadays. I just tell them I'm letting the reindeer rest because tonight's going to be a big night for them."

His grin was contagious, and Gwen found herself smiling wider than she had in a long time. How ridiculous was it that she had a date with Santa? Part of her wanted to take a picture and document the whole thing for the benefit of Jared, who would definitely find this amusing. Another part wanted to keep it to herself.

Life could be horrible, and it could also be wonderful, but one thing was certain—just when you thought you knew what was going to happen next, life proved you wrong.

21

The night air was cold, but both Marina and Stella were bundled for the weather with warm jackets, hats, scarves, and gloves. The fact that they were walking helped too. This was no leisurely stroll—the two of them had a definite destination and were moving at a good clip. But no matter how fast Marina walked, Stella was always a few steps ahead, so excited was she to get to the party.

Marina was glad she'd reconsidered going that night. Too bad if her boss didn't like her fraternizing with the customers. She and Stella were members of the community, and they'd been personally invited by Mrs. Hibbert herself. Judging by how Stella had brightened at the idea of going, this might be the bright spot in their whole Christmas. And Marina sorely needed a bright spot. If Mrs. Krueger begrudged them a bit of extra happiness, it was just too bad.

Stella pointed out the Christmas decorations at various houses along the way. "Look, Mama, the Grinch!" It was indeed the Grinch, along with his beleaguered dog. The figures were nearly life size and not entirely festive, but they put her daughter in the holiday spirit, which was good enough for her.

"I see that."

Two houses down, the façade of a home was completely outlined in lights, including the wide front porch. A spotlight showcased a group of snowmen, actual snowmen, standing in a circle on the lawn, their stick arms reaching out to each other. They had coal eyes and carrot noses and wore vests and top hats. Very old-school. "They're dancing," Stella said, her voice filled with delight.

When they turned the corner, both of them heard the noise at the same time and stopped to listen more closely. Off in the distance came the sound of sleigh bells and what had to be hoof-beats. As they stared in the direction of the noise, a lit-up horse-drawn wagon, driven by Santa, crossed the intersection a block away from where they stood. They'd barely registered what they'd seen when the wagon drove out of sight. "Santa!" Stella shouted joyfully. She pulled on her mother's sleeve. "Did you see him, Mama?"

"I did. I bet he's going to Mrs. Hibbert's. She did say Santa would be there, didn't she?"

Stella's head bobbed in agreement. "She said he's giving out stockings." They continued walking, and then her daughter slowed, moving in step next to her. "I think I might ask him for my Christmas wish." She looked up at her mother with a hopeful expression.

Marina's heart sank. She thought they'd covered this. She exhaled, trying to think of how to stave off what was certain to be a Christmas morning calamity. Casually, she said, "I thought you said you didn't believe in Santa anymore." Marina had never told her Santa didn't exist since she wanted Stella to hold on to her innocence as long as possible, but kids at school talked, and inevitably she'd bumped up against the truth. One of her classmates had told her Santa wasn't real and parents were the ones who bought the gifts. When Stella had asked, her mother had confessed, not wanting to lie. It was inevitable that she'd find out eventually, but it still struck Marina as sad.

"I know there's not a Santa from the North Pole, but the guys who play Santa are real, and Ivy says some of them can do Christmas magic."

Oh, that Ivy. She was a wonderful, sweet little girl, but sometimes Marina wanted to give her a good shake for putting the wrong ideas into Stella's head. "I'm not so sure about that," she said. "The Santa at Mrs. Hibbert's house will be a regular man in a costume, and I'm pretty sure he can't do magic."

Stella's shoulders slumped, and she gave her mom one last beseeching look. "But I can ask him?"

"You can ask if you want. Just don't get your hopes up."

"I won't," she promised.

But even as she said the words, Marina knew it was too late. Stella's hopes were as high as they could be.

22

G wen and Lucky arrived to a flurry of activity. The horses had barely come to a stop when a gaggle of kids, along with their parents, rushed out of Betsy's house to greet them. Lucky immediately went into full-on Santa mode, his white-gloved hand waving in greeting. "Ho, ho, ho!" he cried. "Merry Christmas!" He got out of the wagon and came around to Gwen's side, deftly helping her and Chance get down.

Gwen noticed a younger man with sandy hair quietly approach the wagon and take the reins. "Trent?" When he looked up, she said. "I'm Gwen. It's nice to meet you."

"Nice to meet you too," he said with a shy smile.

Lucky was surrounded now and along with his fans moved in a group toward the house. Gwen and Chance followed. She'd been worried that bringing a dog might cause a disruption, but now she saw that Chance could never overshadow Santa, the rock star of this holiday gathering.

Once inside, she lost sight of him, but a young woman at the door offered to take her coat. "It'll be in the den when you need it," she assured her as Gwen stuffed her gloves in her pockets and her scarf in one sleeve.

Betsy came out then and gave her a big hug. "Gwen! I'm so glad the two of you made it." She stopped to give Chance an affectionate pet. Taking Gwen by the arm, she pulled her into the house, which was now lit up with dozens of strings of Christmas lights. The fireplace was in use, flickering flames giving the room a warm glow. A long table on one side held eating utensils, slow cookers, and platters of food, along with a punch bowl and coffee urn. Beneath the table, a cooler held other beverages. Gwen noticed that most of the furniture had been moved elsewhere, presumably to accommodate the guests who milled around, plates and cups in hand, talking and laughing. Betsy said, "Just make yourself at home and get something to eat. I recommend the apple bread." She winked. "It's delicious." Someone called out Betsy's name, and she excused herself and crossed the room, leaving Gwen behind.

It turned out that Gwen knew more of Poplar Creek's residents than she realized. She recognized Julia, the mail lady; Lucky's sister, Ingrid; Nelson from the bookstore; the veterinarian, Dr. Bach, and his receptionist, Donna; and Betsy's neighbor Kayla, who had her baby, Abbott, in her arms. The little boy, who was sucking on his fingers, looked fairly happy for someone who kept his mother up all night. Others in the crowd looked vaguely familiar. She was sure to have encountered them at one point or another.

Gwen checked over the food table, took a plate, and selected a piece of apple bread. After only one bite she saw the appeal. The bread was spongy, with large chunks of sweet apple throughout. Lucky hadn't been bragging out of turn. His apple bread *was* delicious. The dog looked up at her expectantly, and she felt a wave of guilt for eating in front of him. Everything she'd heard said not to give a dog people food, but certainly it wouldn't hurt just this once? It was Christmas, after all. Surreptitiously, she dropped a large crumb onto the floor right in front of Chance's nose and the dog consumed it in one quick motion.

She was just finishing the last bite of bread when Lucky made his way through the crowd, coming right to her. "Sorry for that," he said, still using his jolly Santa voice. "I didn't mean to leave you behind." He leaned over to acknowledge Chance, his fingers gently going over his head.

"No worries." She waved away his concerns. "I can take care of myself. Besides, I was just noshing on the most divine apple bread."

His face broke into a grin. "You liked it?"

"Loved it."

He adjusted his Santa hat. "I wanted to ask a favor." He leaned in so close she could feel his breath on her cheek. "I'm going to start officially talking to the kids, and I was wondering if you'd hand out the stockings after they're done talking to me. You can be Santa's special assistant."

"Of course. I'd love to." She threw the paper plate into a nearby wastebasket, and then she and Chance followed him out of the living room, guests parting to allow them to pass, little children staring wide-eyed. When they arrived in the next room, she found that what had once been a spacious dining room was now empty of furniture except for one chair backed up in the corner. One very impressive chair.

On second thought, Gwen decided, it was less of a chair and more an ornately carved throne with red leather padding on the seat and back. The distance between the wooden arms was wide. The perfect perch for Santa. Next to the throne was a wooden chest filled with Christmas stockings. Gwen had Chance lie down behind the chair. "Stay," she said, then stood next to the supply of stockings, ready to do her part.

Lucky, as Santa, said in a jolly voice, "Are there any children here who'd like to talk to me?"

Gwen did a quick count and noticed at least ten children and a few babies and toddlers in their mothers' arms, all of them excited to talk to Santa, but none of them the right age and size to be the little girl with the secret Christmas wish. The kids lined up, some of them looking wary, others excited. Lucky had a nice way with the kids, letting them choose their comfort level for the visit.

One little boy named Jayden seemed eager to talk to Santa but didn't want to get too close, so Lucky got down on the floor and sat cross-legged and invited him to sit down as well. Within minutes, Jayden had inched closer, and eventually the two of them were whispering and the boy was giggling. By the time Jayden collected his stocking from Gwen, he was all smiles. "Thank you, Mrs. Claus," he said. She could see why doing this was the best part of Lucky's year.

There were still stockings left when he'd finished with all the chats and picture taking, but Gwen supposed it was better to wind up with extra than potentially shortchange a child. Lucky stepped away from his throne to talk to a parent who was asking if he was available for hire for parties. As he was explaining that he didn't take money for being Santa, Gwen peeked inside one of the stockings to see what she'd been handing out. She was so preoccupied checking out the candy, sugar cookie, bookmark, and small stuffed animal that she almost didn't hear a little girl's voice saying, "Santa, can I talk to you? It's important."

With a start, she looked up to see a girl of seven or eight with dark shoulder-length hair tugging on Lucky's sleeve. Mentally she flashed back to the bookstore and the day she'd witnessed the origami star being hung on the tree. Her heart fluttered in excitement as she realized this girl fit the description. Lucky said, "Of course, my child. Come with me." He walked back to the throne, his hand on her shoulder. He said, "Would you like to take a seat?" and when she sat down, he knelt next to her.

"It's like this, Santa," she said, her eyes wide. "My friend Ivy says sometimes even fake Santas can do real magic."

Lucky nodded. "I see. What sort of magic are we talking about?"

Gwen found herself inching closer, trying to hear over the noise of the party. She tried to dart a look at Lucky that said, *Ask her name!* but his attention was solely on the little girl.

"I made a wish for a gift for my mom on a star," she said, lowering her voice, "because I wanted her to get something special for Christmas, but my mom said it won't work and that someone at the bookstore threw out my wish."

Gwen knew the exact moment when Lucky put it together because his eyes widened and a smile stretched across his face. "Well, Stella," he said, "I think I know what it is you asked for." He beckoned for her to come closer and then whispered in her ear. When he pulled away, he said, "Did I get it right?"

"Yes," she whispered, astonished. "And how did you know my name?"

Lucky said, "I know a great many things."

The answer seemed to satisfy her. She said, "My wish is really important because now our oven is broken, and my mom cried about it. She said everything has been going wrong lately."

"I see." He nodded in a knowing way.

"So can you make my Christmas wish come true?" she asked, studying his face.

"I can't make any promises. There are so many children and so many wishes in the world," Lucky said, "but I can tell this is important to you, so I will do my very best."

A satisfied smile crossed her lips. "Thank you, Santa."

"Is there anything you want for yourself, Stella?" Lucky laced his fingers together. "A toy or a book? Some clothes, maybe?"

"No, I'm good. Thanks." She scooted to the front edge of the throne and hopped down. "Just the wish I wanted for my mom. That will be enough." She quickly reached out and gave him a hug before turning to walk away. She would have left without her stocking if Gwen hadn't held it out in her line of sight. "Thank you, Mrs. Claus," she said, taking it from her hand.

As Stella walked away, she glanced back over her shoulder to say one last thing. "Don't forget."

Lucky said, "I won't."

❦ 23 ❦

Marina hadn't planned on getting separated from her daughter at the Christmas party, but Stella wanted to see Santa, and Mrs. Hibbert insisted on introducing her to her neighbor in the kitchen, and so, against her better judgment, she let Stella go off on her own. "Come find me when you're done," she'd said.

"She'll be fine," Mrs. Hibbert assured her, leading her down a hallway to the kitchen. Out in the main room, the sound of conversation and Christmas music filled the air, but the back of the house was quieter. An older lady peered into the refrigerator, while another stood at the counter, cutting vegetables on a wooden board. A third woman, a young mother, sat at the table, a baby held up against one cloth-diaper-covered shoulder.

It was this woman that Betsy addressed. She clasped her hands together and said, "Kayla, the cavalry has arrived!" Gesturing to Marina, she said, "This is Marina, the lady I told you about. I can absolutely vouch for her. Marina, this is my neighbor Kayla, and the little one is her son, Abbott. Kayla is desperate for help with the baby, and you said you were looking for some work over the next few weeks, and I thought to myself, *This is a match made in heaven.* Believe me, you two are going to get along beautifully." She pulled out a chair and gestured to Marina. "I'll leave you to it."

Marina sat down as Mrs. Hibbert left the room. She wasn't sure what to say, but as it turned out, Kayla did all the talking. "I'm so worn out I can't stand it," she said, rubbing the baby's back. "He's quiet now, but the minute I try to set him down he'll be wide awake. And screaming. Boy, can he scream." She went on and on, talking about her frustration and how tired she was. "I don't expect anyone to work at night, but if I could get some help during the day, it would help my sanity. Sometimes I really feel like I'm losing it. Most days I'd give my pinkie finger for a nap." Getting down to business, she mentioned an hourly rate that was nearly twice what Marina got for cleaning and then said, "Could you work twenty hours a week?" When Marina hesitated, she hurriedly amended it. "Or less if you can't do that much. Anything would help."

Marina sat up straight and mentally did the math. It sounded as if she could work around her current schedule. "I think I could manage twenty hours. Can I bring my daughter along when she's not in school?"

"How old is she?"

"She's eight and loves babies. And she's very well behaved."

"Of course. That would be fine."

Mrs. Hibbert returned with a glass of punch and a plate of food. She set both down in front of Marina. "So what do you think, girls? Am I the best matchmaker in the world or what?"

"If Marina agrees to take the job, I would agree with that." Kayla shifted Abbott to the other shoulder.

"I would love to help you out," Marina said.

"Can you start the day after Christmas?"

"Absolutely."

Kayla gave a sigh of relief. "Thank God." She turned to Betsy.

"I'll give it to you, then. Betsy, you're officially the best match-maker in the world."

"I knew it," Betsy said triumphantly.

After Betsy left the room, they kept talking over the details. Marina felt the lifting of her spirits. The oven wasn't fixed yet and the bills were still coming in, but knowing she had this added income on the horizon assuaged her worry. By the time Kayla decided to head for home, they'd exchanged phone numbers and worked out a schedule for the next few weeks.

Marina had just finished the food on her plate and was getting up to find her daughter when Stella dashed in through the door, a Christmas stocking in her hand. "Mama, guess what?"

"What, my darling?"

"That Santa is the kind Ivy was talking about!" Her face shone with excitement. "He knew all about my wish, and he knew my name too."

Marina decided right then that she wasn't going to squash Stella's good mood. There was no way the man playing Santa knew her wish, and as for knowing her name? No doubt someone at the party had clued him in, or maybe he'd overheard someone call her by name. No matter. Getting a new job seemed like a Christmas miracle already. She would let Stella believe for just a little longer. "That's wonderful!"

"Can we go home now?"

"You want to leave?"

"Yes, please."

Marina thought about the cold walk home ahead of them and how early Stella would be awakening in the morning, and heading home early sounded just about right. "Of course," she said. "Let me say goodbye to Mrs. Hibbert, and then we can go."

❦ 24 ❦

After Stella walked away, Gwen sidled up to Lucky. "I can't believe we did it." She gave his arm a squeeze. "After everything we tried, she just walked into the room."

"She didn't just walk into the room," he said. "It's Christmas magic. There's nothing like it."

She thought it was more coincidence than magic but wasn't going to contradict him. The important thing was that they'd found her. "Now what?" she said.

Before he could answer, a woman approached, guiding a boy who looked to be about kindergarten age. "See, Santa's still here." She guided her son toward Lucky. "Go ahead. Don't be shy."

Lucky backed up into the chair and became Santa once again, talking to the child, whose name turned out to be Noah, and listening intently to Noah's extensive list of wants. When the boy stopped to take a breath, Lucky said, "I'm so glad you shared your list with me." Gwen could tell he was trying to wrap things up, but Noah's mother got in the act, telling Santa all about her son's recent transgressions, as if Santa might be able to help. "We all make mistakes," Lucky said. "The important thing is that we try to do better. Now, Noah, if you go over to my helper, Gwen, she'll give you a stocking full of goodies."

By the time Noah and his mother walked away, Gwen had freed Chance's leash from the chair and had the loop in her hand. "So, what's the plan?" she asked.

"Now we ask Betsy for Stella's last name or address." His face looked flushed, giving him a nice rosy glow. Like a real Santa. "And then we give a little girl her wish."

But when they asked Betsy, she had a blank look on her face. "Stella? Doesn't sound familiar." She scanned the room for the girl, and so did they, but Stella wasn't in sight.

Lucky tried again, holding out his hand, palm facing downward. "She's about this tall? Dark hair, shoulder length, cute as can be?"

"Oh!" Betsy's face lit up. "That has to be Marina's daughter. I don't think I caught her name. They just left a few minutes ago."

Gwen stepped closer, leaning in. "Do you know where they live?"

Betsy shook her head. "Close by, I think. I always see the two of them walking around here."

"What's Marina's last name?" Lucky asked.

She twisted her lips in thought, but it was clear from the look on her face that she didn't know. Gwen said, "It's really important. Lucky and I want to grant Stella's Christmas wish."

"I'm sorry," Betsy said finally. "I don't know. She works for the company that cleans my house twice a month. That's how we met." Thoughtfully, she held her fist to her chin. "You know, my neighbor Kayla might know how to find her. Marina is going to do some childcare for her in the next few weeks. Let me call Kayla for you." She gestured for them to follow her, leading them to the den, where it was quieter. Once there, she pulled out her cell phone and made the call, putting it on speaker.

When Kayla answered, they heard a baby wailing in the background. After Betsy explained the situation, Kayla said, "I'm sorry I don't have her address or last name, just her phone number."

Lucky jotted down the phone number. Better than nothing, Gwen thought, but she couldn't even imagine how that would help. They were complete strangers. It wasn't like they could call and ask where she lived. No one would give out information like that over the phone.

After Betsy ended the call, she asked, "Does that help?"

"It certainly does," Lucky said with a smile. "On that note, Gwen, I think it's time for Santa to leave."

It wasn't until they were back in Santa's sleigh and heading down the street that Gwen asked, "So you know how to get an address from a cell phone number?"

Lucky shook his head. "No, I don't."

"Oh." What a letdown. "So we're just giving up?" A light snow began to come down, swirling all around them. She remembered standing outside as a kid during snowfalls like this and opening her mouth to catch snowflakes on her tongue.

"Not giving up so much as rethinking it." He gave the reins a little shake, and the horses quickened their pace.

"My son might know a way to find out an address from a cell number." The younger generation knew the ins and outs of the internet much better than their parents.

"That's a good thought." The words were positive, but Lucky sounded defeated.

Gwen didn't blame him. She felt that way herself. They'd come so close, actually talked to Stella, and yet, without more information, they still couldn't fulfill her Christmas wish. The mood of the evening dampened, she sat quietly, the jingling bells and horses' hooves clopping on the pavement the only sounds punctuating the night air. They passed houses with bright lights and festive lawn displays, but the sight no longer filled her heart with gladness. Chance, too, seemed to have run out of energy, curled up at her feet, his eyes closed.

She didn't mind a Christmas disappointment for herself, but now that she'd seen that little girl's face lit up with joy at the thought of her mother getting a new washer and dryer, she couldn't bear the thought that they were going to let her down.

On the way home, Stella swung her newly acquired Christmas stocking from side to side as she walked. Her steps were buoyant, her attitude jubilant. "I think we're going to have the best Christmas ever, Mama!"

Flakes swirled down around them. "I hope so," Marina said, her voice guarded. Whatever the party Santa had promised, she was sure it wasn't going to happen, but it was out of her hands now. Stella was more likely to believe Santa over her mother when it came to Christmas magic. "But no matter what happens, we'll have fun. We'll be together, open some gifts, and have a special dinner. We'll be calling your grandparents too."

From somewhere behind them they heard the jingle of bells and the clip-clopping of horses' hooves. The party Santa. Marina wanted to hunt him down and give him a piece of her mind for getting her child's hopes up, but that certainly wasn't the holiday spirit. Stella stopped and turned, and then Marina glanced back and saw it too—the sleigh on wheels heading their way.

They were stock-still on the sidewalk when Santa called out, "Whoa, there! Whoa, boys," and the sleigh came to a stop right next to them. He leaned down and said, "Why, if it isn't Stella and her mother! Can we offer you a ride home?"

They were only a few minutes away from home, and if Marina had been alone she would have declined, but one look at Stella's face and it was impossible to say no. Santa climbed down and assisted them up to the bench seat in back, and Stella said, "Mama, this is Mrs. Claus, and oh look, they have a dog!"

Mrs. Claus, who didn't look old enough or dressed for the part, turned around and said, "The dog's name is Chance, and I'm Gwen." She handed back a thick velour blanket.

Marina took the blanket and covered Stella's legs. "It's a pleasure to meet you," she said. "I'm Marina, and you know Stella. We only live about three blocks away, on Bedford Lane. We're nearly home, so I'm sorry to trouble you."

"Ho, ho, ho," Santa said. "No trouble at all." He hopped back up front, surprisingly nimble and quick, jiggled the reins, and said, "Giddy up!"

Stella bounced in her seat, unable to contain her excitement. Marina, despite her irritation that the party Santa had made promises to her daughter, had to admit that a sleigh ride with Santa was an unexpected Christmas Eve treat. When Stella stood up and began chattering away to Santa and Mrs. Claus, showing them where her friend Ivy lived and pointing out the way to her house, Marina couldn't help from smiling. Other parents might have thought they had the best daughter ever, but those people were wrong. She was the one blessed with Stella, which meant she had the best daughter ever.

When they pulled up in front of their house, Santa hopped down to help them out of the sleigh. "Merry Christmas!" he said, loud enough that his voice carried down the block.

"Merry Christmas, Santa!" Stella said as he lifted her down to the ground.

From the front porch, Marina and Stella waved goodbye. "I

told him not to forget," Stella said once the sleigh had turned the corner and was out of sight, "and he said he wouldn't."

Marina put her arm around her daughter's shoulders. "We'll see."

❧ 26 ❧

D*ecember 25*

IF GWEN HAD MADE A LIST OF ALL THE THINGS SHE MIGHT possibly be doing on Christmas Day, delivering appliances would not have been on it. And yet, here she was at eight in the morning, sitting in the front seat of Lucky's car, waiting for his friend Blake to show up. Chance was with Ingrid, who'd offered to dogsit while they fulfilled Stella's wish. She thought of what Ingrid had told her the day they'd met up in the bookstore. *Just listen to your intuition. It will steer you in the right direction.* She hadn't been wrong.

After they'd dropped off Marina and Stella the night before, both of them had been excited to finally have an address. "Now we know where to have the washer and dryer delivered," Gwen said as the sleigh pulled away. "Too bad we can't get them in time for Christmas."

"Who says we can't?" Lucky raised his eyebrows.

Gwen said, "Do you know an appliance store that delivers on Christmas?"

"Even better. I know an appliance store guy who owes me a favor."

The next morning, they'd parked down the block, trying not to arouse suspicion in the neighborhood, which was challenging since Lucky was once again in full Santa regalia. He'd also brought a Mrs. Claus hat for Gwen to wear, which she'd gladly donned even though it smashed down her hair. With a jolt, she suddenly realized that she hadn't checked Shawna's Instagram in two days and had zero interest in knowing what she and Dean were doing for the holiday. She glanced over at Lucky and couldn't suppress a giggle.

"You find this amusing?" he said with a smile.

"I'm just happy. So very happy." This was the honest truth. She'd gone from Christmas misery to complete joy in the space of a week and now found that the future looked brighter than she'd ever imagined.

When a white appliance truck pulled up in front of Stella's house, Lucky said, "That's our cue. We're on."

Gwen felt happiness bubble up from inside her as she and Lucky made their way down the sidewalk. Ahead of them, Blake had already pulled up the back door of the truck and lowered the ramp. A stainless-steel washer and dryer were inside, along with a new oven. All of them were topped with a red bow as large as a laundry basket. Seeing them approach, Blake said, "Only for you, Lucky. There's not another man alive who could get me to do this on Christmas morning."

Lucky laughed. "Yeah, like you don't owe me a hundred favors." He put his arm around Gwen's shoulders. "Meet Gwen, my new partner in crime."

Blake tipped his cap, "Nice to meet you, Gwen! You should know that this guy is trouble."

"I'm counting on it," she said with a laugh.

Blake pulled out a dolly and positioned it under the washer, then wheeled it down the ramp and over the curb. Lucky and Gwen walked ahead of him, and when they got to the front door, Lucky pointed silently, indicating she should do the honors. She pressed the doorbell and felt giddy upon hearing it ring inside. When Marina opened the door, Stella was next to her, bouncing on her heels.

"Merry Christmas!" Lucky said. "I have a special present for Stella's mother!" He and Gwen stepped aside to reveal the washer. The expression on Marina's face was not outright surprise, like Gwen had expected. Instead, she looked puzzled and a bit taken aback.

"Excuse me?"

"It's a new washer, just for you," Gwen said, "and there's a dryer and an oven too!"

Lucky said, "Merry Christmas! We're delivering gifts from Stella."

"I told you, Mama, didn't I tell you?" Stella's excitement came from pure selfless jubilation. "I told you Santa would come with a surprise."

Marina looked from her daughter to the visitors on her front porch, and her face slowly widened into a smile. "This washer is for me?"

"Yes, it's for you!" Gwen said. "Your daughter put in a request on your behalf. She's a very special little girl."

Marina leaned over to kiss the top of Stella's head. "I know that. I'm very lucky." She stepped back and opened the door wide to allow them to come in. "I'm sorry for my reaction. I'm just floored. I didn't expect this at all."

"Now we don't have to walk to the laundromat anymore," Stella said. "I made a wish on a Christmas star, and it came true, Mama!"

As Blake maneuvered the washer over the threshold, Lucky said in his Santa voice, "Mrs. Claus and I can't stay. As you can imagine, today's a busy day for us, but we wanted to stop in and thank Stella for helping us out." He held up his palm, and Stella gave him a high five. "Blake here will install the washer and dryer and oven for you. If you have any questions, he's the man to ask."

"I can't thank you enough," Marina said. "I'm in complete shock. I was afraid that Stella would be disappointed this morning. I had no idea she asked for something for me."

"No need to thank us. It was your daughter's greatest Christmas wish that you get something special. She wants you to be happy," Gwen said, blinking back tears. "Merry Christmas!"

After they exchanged their goodbyes, Gwen and Lucky made their way back to the car. "That went well," he said. "You know I'm still going to have to pick another winner for a washer and dryer at the laundromat, but I'd say it's worth it."

"Thank goodness we happened to see them walking home last night," Gwen responded. "That was a lucky coincidence."

Lucky shook his head. "It wasn't a coincidence. It was Christmas magic."

"Christmas magic." Gwen repeated the words, but this time the concept didn't seem so far-fetched. "Now that we've done one Christmas good deed, what did you have planned for the rest of the day?"

"I want to hit up a nursing home. Are you interested in accompanying me as my date?"

"Believe me, Santa, there's no place I'd rather be."

ONCE THE WASHER AND DRYER HAD BEEN INSTALLED AND THE oven switched out, Marina and Stella bid goodbye to Blake and watched as he drove away. Afterward, Marina made hot chocolate for the two of them to drink in the living room near the tree. Stella took a candy cane off the tree, unwrapped it, and dropped it into her mug, the curve hooked over the rim. "Were you surprised, Mama? Were you really and truly surprised?" she asked, sitting cross-legged on the floor in front of the nativity scene.

"I was really and truly surprised," Marina said, setting her mug on a coaster on the coffee table. "So, all this time, when you made the origami star and when you had your window open that night looking for falling stars, you were making a wish for me?"

Stella bobbed her head in a yes. "I wanted it so bad. I knew it would make you happy."

One day ago, Marina had been sick with worry over their money situation and Stella's Christmas expectations. And now, just like that, her troubles were gone. Maybe there was something to Christmas wishes after all.

※ 27 ※

T *hirteen months later*

UNDERNEATH THE SHADE OF A CABANA, GWEN SAT BACK IN HER lounge chair, taking in the ocean view. The sight of gentle waves caressing white sand was relaxing. Off in the distance, a speedboat raced through the water, pulling a man and woman parasailing in tandem, a rainbow-colored parachute keeping them airborne. Down the beach to her right, two children laughed in the shallow water, their parents keeping a watchful eye on them. Earlier in the day, Gwen had taken a picture of the beach and sent it to Jared with a text that said: *Greetings from paradise*. He'd sent back a smiling emoji.

When her phone rang, she assumed it was Jared, so it was a shock to see her ex-husband's name on the screen. She put it on speaker. "Hello?" The only reason Dean might be calling was if something had happened to their son. *Oh no. Anything but that.*

"Gwen, how are you doing?"

She ignored the question. "Is Jared okay?"

"As far as I know." Dean sounded amused. "Look, I know you must be surprised to hear from me, but I'm doing some traveling and will be near Poplar Creek tomorrow. I was wondering if you'd be able to meet me for lunch."

"Meet you for lunch?" She couldn't keep the incredulous note out of her voice.

"Or dinner, if that's better."

"You want me to go out to eat with you and Shawna?" There was a long pause, so silent that she thought they might have been disconnected, but then she heard him clear his throat.

Dean said, "I'm not with Shawna anymore, actually."

"Oh, I'm sorry."

"Don't be. It was just one of those things. It ran its course. You understand."

Just one of those things. He'd upended her life for a relationship that lacked durability and substance. She exhaled. "So why did you want to get together?"

"I thought we could talk about old times. I really miss you, Gwen."

She glanced up to see Lucky heading her way, a tropical drink in each hand. He set the umbrella-garnished glasses on the table between them, then sat on the edge of his chair, giving her a quizzical look. Gwen said, "Well, I can't meet you for lunch or dinner, because I'm not actually in Poplar Creek. I'm on vacation."

"Maybe when you get back?" He sounded wistful.

"I'm sorry, Dean, but I'd rather not get together with you. I'm grateful for our son and the years we had together, but I've moved on. I wish you the best."

"Oh." He clearly wasn't expecting that response. "Well, if you reconsider, the offer is open."

"I'll keep that in mind. Thanks. Bye." When she looked up, Lucky had a twinkle in his eye. "What?"

"I feel a little sorry for the guy. He sounded very sad."

"His happiness is not my problem anymore."

Lucky sat back and clapped his sand-covered feet together. "You're right about that." After a moment, he said, "When I was at the bar getting the drinks, Marina sent me a video. You want to see it?"

"I do." She and Lucky had kept up with Marina and Stella after that fateful Christmas Day. Things had really turned around for the mother and daughter in the last year. With the help of Lucky's mentorship and a small business loan, Marina had started her own company, Marina's Helping Hands, and had gotten so busy she'd recently hired one other woman to keep up with the demand. Marina and Stella were the first ones Gwen had thought of when they needed a dog-sitter for this vacation. Fortunately, they'd happily agreed to take the job.

Lucky handed her the phone. When Gwen clicked on the video, she saw Chance playing fetch with Stella. It looked like he was having the time of his life, running and leaping and barking happily. Clearly, he was adjusting well to her absence. "Little traitor," she said, setting the phone on the table.

Lucky got to his feet and pointed. "Look up."

Gwen glanced up to see mistletoe dangling from the overhang of the cabana. She tilted her head to one side. "Hmm, I wonder how that got up there?"

Lucky knelt down next to her, pulled out a ring box, and snapped it open. As she spotted the gorgeous diamond ring shimmering in the light, her hand went to her heart.

She said, "Is this . . . ?"

He nodded. "Gwen Hayward, the last year has been the happiest of my life. You have a big heart and make everything more fun, whether it's a stop at the gas station or a beach vacation. I can't imagine being Santa without you as Mrs. Claus, and I love you beyond measure. Would you do me the honor of letting me be your husband?"

She smiled, tears welling up in her eyes. "Yes, I would."

"Oh, thank God," he said with a laugh. "If you'd said no, it would have made the rest of the vacation so awkward." He took the ring out of the box and slipped it on her ring finger, then sat on the edge of her chair and kissed her.

And as she kissed him right back with the mistletoe hanging above their heads, it occurred to her that Christmas magic, the kind that brought happily-ever-afters, made dreams come true every day of the year.

LUCKY'S APPLE BREAD RECIPE

3 cups all-purpose flour
    2 teaspoons cinnamon
    1 teaspoon baking soda
    ½ teaspoon baking powder
    ½ teaspoon salt
    ½ cup vegetable oil
    2 cups sugar
    2 eggs, beaten
    ½ teaspoon vanilla
    2 cups apples, peeled, cored, coarsely chopped
    1 cup broken walnuts (optional)

In bowl, combine flour, cinnamon, baking soda, baking powder, and salt; set aside. In large mixing bowl, stir together oil, sugar, eggs, vanilla, and apples. Stir into flour mixture. Add walnuts and mix. Divide mixture* between two greased 8×4-inch bread pans.

Bake at 350 degrees for 40–45 minutes or until breads test done.

Cool for 10 minutes on wire rack before removing from pans.

Yield: 2 loaves

*Mixture will be very thick, almost like cookie dough. If necessary, mix the batter with clean hands. It's a goopy mess but worth it for the end result!

ACKNOWLEDGMENTS

A million thanks to editor Jessica Fogleman, whose attention to detail is astounding. I appreciate her professionalism and expertise more than I can say. I also owe a debt of gratitude to Michelle San Juan, who gave me valuable feedback and reassurance just when I needed it.

A wave of gratitude and hugs to the following early readers (in no particular order): Elaine Sapp, Sheri Powers, Kathy Aden, Lisa Wetzel, Marie L. Lappin, Phyllis Jones Pisanelli, Keenalynn Pratt, Katie Waddell, Ann Marie Gruszkowski, Pat Tarter, Carol Zuba, Amy Barbaro Coats, Tammy Morse, Gabrielle Land Read, Rhonda Sedgwick, and MaryAnn Schaefer. I appreciate each and every one of you.

As always, I'm indebted to my wonderful husband, Greg, and our kids, Charlie, Rachel, Maria, and Jack. Every day I'm showered with more love and support than I deserve.

And last, but never least, a big thank-you to the readers of my books. What can I say? I'm so privileged to be able to write stories for a living, and I never take my readers for granted. I appreciate each and every one of you and doubly so if you leave a review or recommend one of my books to others. Here's hoping all of you get your own Christmas magic.

Made in United States
North Haven, CT
08 May 2022

18966973R00093